A Christian Military Romance

A Soldier Finds Grace

Katherine St. Clair

MAPLEWOOD
— PUBLISHING —

Contents

Chapter One

They'd been in France, Luxembourg, Belgium, and had now crossed the line into Germany. It was almost dark when they came into camp. Matthew Finley, Jr. and William Sawyer had come in dirty and hungry. There had been soldiers here before them. Many American lives had already been lost in the soil that they now placed their boots on.

The two had just put their packs by their Army cots. Matthew's daily ration had run out hours before, and since they'd been travelling almost entirely on foot, his appetite had started talking to him again almost immediately after he had eaten the last of his rations.

"There's the field kitchen. Hot food is the best thing I can think of next to sleep," William said, sitting on his cot across from Matthew.

William was twenty-one, just like Matthew. The two had gotten along right from the start.

"I can't decide if I'd rather just lay down right now or if my stomach is pushy enough to get me in front of a plate of hot food," Matthew said as he unlaced the tops of his boots to give his ankles a few minutes to breathe.

"Food, that's my vote. Then sleep," William looked around at all their fellow soldiers settling into the tent.

Wilbur Archer, certainly the most spirited man in their platoon, had just taken up a song about corned beef and spam.

"The days when I had a pot roast beside me are gone with the days of sweet toast and honey. I've sat in the fields eating only the canned, and now I will feast on corned beef and spam—"

Wilbur had a deep baritone that he displayed whenever possible, which was not very often on the battlefield. The men had been pushing the front forward, and now they were once again close to battle.

"Can't you turn that down?" William asked Matthew as he gestured to Wilbur. Wilbur gave a grin that exposed a gap in his lower teeth. A tooth had recently been knocked free when Wilbur had fallen face first into a stationary tank.

"You're right, I can't," Matthew laughed at Wilbur's enthusiasm, then stood next to William as they walked back out of the tent. He felt light, walking without a pack on. He hadn't laced his boots back up, which made him tread carefully so as not to trip over himself. He would have walked barefoot if his platoon commander would had allowed it.

The three walked to the field kitchen tent where a line was growing. No one spoke as they waited, too tired from the long haul they had taken to get there. The smell of meat stew kept them from turning back to their tent where they could sit or lie down. When they'd made it through the line and sat down, the men ate hungrily.

Matthew knew he should slow down, but he couldn't force himself to do it. It was too good, and he was too hungry.

"You didn't pray," Wilbur said. "You always pray before you eat."

Matthew was surprised that Wilbur had noticed. He didn't do it for anyone else to notice. He said a quick prayer silently before eating most every meal.

"I prayed while I was in line so I could I get to eating faster," Matthew smiled at Wilbur, who laughed.

"I've heard a lot of guys have died here already," Wilbur said after taking a few more bites. His face had gone serious, and Matthew swallowed his bite.

"We're close to the front," William said as he cleaned off the last scrapes of food from his plate.

"I know we are," Wilbur said without looking up. "Did you see all those tarps we walked by? There were bodies underneath them."

"They would send the bodies back," Matthew looked at Wilbur.

"Don't have room. Too busy bringing in fresh men."

William was looking at Wilbur now too, and he turned to exchange a look with Matthew.

"The guy I talked to said he lost his whole company, only him and two other guys made it back alive."

Matthew had already cleared his plate, but now he wished he hadn't. His appetite was going sour quickly. Matthew turned his gaze up.

"Praying again?" Wilbur asked.

"No," Matthew gave a little puff of breath. "Just looking at the trees."

Both Wilbur and William looked up into the trees as well. There were plenty of trees where Matthew had come from in North Carolina. He'd always felt more at peace with the world when there was nature nearby. Even now with the threat of battle on the horizon, Matthew took comfort in the green.

"Cold out here," Wilbur said, standing. The two other men stood with him.

"You eat?" Tom O'Brien, their platoon leader, put a heavy hand on Matthew's shoulder.

"Yes, sir."

"Good, I need you and Sawyer to come with me," Tom turned just as quickly as he'd come upon them. Matthew looked at William. William shrugged and gave a small two-fingered wave to Wilbur who seemed happy not to be included.

Matthew fought the urge to ask what the interruption was about and when they'd be able to go back to their tent to get some sleep. He looked down at his partially unlaced boots and now wished he'd left them tied.

"Sawyer, Finley," Tom O'Brien held out a hand to issue them into a private tent. Matthew's heartbeat picked up. Had he done something wrong? Had something bad happened at home? If it had to do with home, then William wouldn't be with him so it couldn't be that. No, they must have done something.

"Private Finley, Private Sawyer," Tom O'Brien motioned to the man in front of them. Matthew already had his hand up in a salute, and William's was fast ascending. "Colonel Swenson."

"Sir," Matthew said in sync with William. From the corner of his eye, Matthew could see Tony Paulson, one of the other guys from their platoon, standing by.

"At ease, soldiers," Colonel Swenson was sitting at a desk with his a thick cigarette lit and smoking from a small ashtray that sat next to his right hand. "I've called you in today on O'Brien's recommendation. There is something particular I would like to do, and you three seem the best suited for the task."

The Colonel took a moment to compose his thoughts and then looked back up, "We have lost a lot of men in the last few days. It...well, it's been a bloodbath for our men. We are running out of gas, we need to replenish our ammunition. We've been pushing hard since we came in at Normandy, and now I think we're at a pivotal point in our operations."

The Colonel looked from Matthew to William and then to Tony.

"O'Brien, would you care to tell the men what we've been talking about?"

Matthew looked at O'Brien, who was standing stiff at attention in a way Matthew had never seen the man do before. O'Brien saluted the Colonel, "Yes, sir."

He turned to Matthew, William, and Tony and a knowing look passed from his eyes to each of theirs. He'd been with them for a long time and knew who they were and what they stood for.

"We've decided to send in a small group of men to get some information. We need to know where the Germans are and where their ammunition is held. We will use the information to plan an attack on their least-covered ammo stockpile. We can bring their weapons back with us and use it to continue the fight. We can't give up any ground now. We've come too far."

Matthew nodded, understanding vaguely what O'Brien was telling them.

"You want us to go in, sir?" William asked and Matthew could hear the questions in his voice. *Why us?*

"Exactly," O'Brien looked at each of them again. "Tony is the best sniper I've got. Once we find out where we will attack, Tony will help to disarm them quickly so we can go in and get out fast. You," he said, pointing to William, "speak German"

"Not well, sir," William's voice was full of hesitation.

"I just need you to understand it. If there's anything to be heard, then you'll report back to us. Finley, you'll mark everything you see on the map."

Matthew was good with maps, very good. He'd been doing most of the navigation for his company since he'd pointed out a problem early on. His ingrained sense of direction had tipped him off to a potential catastrophe in France. The entire company had been headed in the wrong direction, straight for a potential fatal encounter across the enemy line, which would have resulted in disaster. With Matthew's correction, the catastrophe had been averted.

After that, Matthew had been asked to look over their company's maps before they moved forward. He'd never particularly considered himself much of a navigator. It was just something his mind processed well. To put him in charge of something like this felt like a stretch.

"Are you sure, sir, I don't have any formal training"

"I'm sure," O'Brien smiled grimly at Matthew.

Matthew nodded and turned to the Colonel, "I'll do my best, sir."

"Good, we are losing men too quickly out here. With a map of German activity, we could do a lot to prevent the unnecessary loss of more lives."

"Going in the morning, sir?" William asked.

"Tonight. We want the cover of darkness. I know you're tired, but I think it's best that we move right away."

William nodded for all three of them.

On their way back to their tent, all four men were silent. O'Brien was bringing up the back, and William was leading the way.

"You men collect your things. You'll go in carrying only what you need. You want to be as mobile as possible." O'Brien paused. "I think it would be best to write a note home before you go."

Matthew looked to William, whose jaw tightened. They were being told pointblank that there was a good chance they wouldn't make it back alive. They were about to walk right into the enemy camp. "We'll meet here in twenty," O'Brien said, looking at the ground. There was a serious feeling flowing among all of them, and a heaviness was settling down on Matthew's shoulders.

"Hey, what did you get called out for?" Wilbur walked over to Matthew and William. Tony's cot was a row away.

"Nothing much," William smiled. "Go catch some shuteye. I'm going write home."

Wilbur looked to Matthew.

"Me too," Matthew said.

Wilbur looked between the two, then turned and looked at Tony who had come in with them. Tony had the same serious look creasing his face, and Wilbur turned back.

"Godspeed," he said, suddenly looking as serious as the three of them. "Come back safe."

Matthew didn't know how Wilbur understood, or how much he understood, but he nodded at the other man as he pulled out a pencil, two envelopes, and two sheets of paper.

Wilbur went back to his cot, but Matthew could still feel the other man's eyes on him.

When he was done, he folded the sheets and placed them each in an addressed envelope and took them out to O'Brien. Matthew handed him both letters, then watched as William and Tony made their way out and did the same.

"There's no smoking tonight, so you can leave your cigarettes here," O'Brien said. He pulled out mapping tools for Matthew and a notebook for William. Tony crossed himself, and O'Brien turned to Matthew.

"I think, Finley, we could all use a prayer tonight. Would you do the honors?"

Matthew was only surprised for a second by the request, then quickly nodded, "Of course." Matthew bowed his head and felt the others do the same.

"Lord, we ask for your protection tonight as we make our way out into enemy territory. We ask you to guide our steps as we look for information that will help our fellow soldiers. Help us to be brave, and to find what we are looking for. Be with my companions, and be with my enemies. Let all of them know you. Walk with us, Lord. Amen." Matthew opened his eyes to the gazes of William, Tony, and O'Brien.

"We'll go then," O'Brien said nodding in Matthew's direction.

Chapter Two

"Did you see all the men who are still outside waiting to be brought in? We'll be here all night—" Millie Davis put out her hand to take the newly sanitized surgical equipment Grace was handing to her.

"Here we go," Grace took a deep breath and briefly thought about the long chaotic night that lay ahead. Millie moved off to the surgery that had been put up just in time for their first casualties.

The whole group had only just finished putting up the field hospital. They'd spent thirteen days in their last location before taking down the tents, cots, and equipment and moving them behind the soldiers as they moved their line forward.

Now, almost immediately, all of the cots in the main tent were full, and soldiers were waiting, burned, broken, and in shock, outside.

"Grace, we need you at receiving," Eileen, the platoon chief nurse, said as she walked past Grace. Grace immediately moved in step with Eileen, running a bit to catch up. "You take down names and injuries. I want to know who needs to get into surgery first, who needs to move to shock. Got it?"

"Yes, ma'am."

"I'll take these men, you take everyone from here," Eileen motioned, "back."

Grace nodded and immediately moved to the first man who looked in immediate need of surgery.

"Name," Grace tried not to look at the open gash in the young soldier's head. She could see the white of skull. Grace wondered where the man's helmet was.

"Charlie Dunn, Private, Second Class, from Jackson, Mississippi," The boy's voice was light and high-pitched. He sounded as young as he looked. Grace wrote the boy's name down and took a note about his head and what she could see.

"What happened, Charlie?"

"Grenade went off right next to me. My friend, Gerald Slaton, he was blown up." He said it as if he were still watching it, eyes glazing over, looking into the floor. Grace watched his eyes and made a note about Gerald Slaton.

"Ok, we're going to get you into surgery soon." Grace put her face in Charlie Dunn's line of vision. The young man nodded, and Grace looked around her.

Men were everywhere. Blood, dirt, and body heat were beginning to flow through the room. Grace felt overwhelmed. *Lord, protect these boys*, she said in a quick prayer as her eyes skimmed the faces. She noted that some of these faces didn't even have facial hair yet.

Grace quickly moved to a man whose left arm from the elbow down had been blown off. A tourniquet had already been applied. Grace bent over him, examining the wound.

"Name?" She had begun to hit her stride. She could feel the adrenaline pushing through her body, encouraging her forward, making her mind work faster.

"Corporal Harold Hackley," The man said through clenched teeth. He was barely conscious.

"Hello, Harold. We are going to take care of you today. In just a few minutes, we'll have you in surgery. Ok?"

Harold gave a half-inch nod.

"Where are you from Harold?"

"Pine Bluff, Arkansas, ma'am." It was obviously so hard for Harold to speak that Grace felt a little guilty.

"A good Arkansas boy, made of hardy stuff. You'll be just fine, Harold." Grace stood up and moved to the next man.

She handed off the intake sheets to Eileen as she went until she was called to switch places with a nurse in post-op. It was seven hours before the fast pace slowed down. Grace knew it would be much longer before she could think about taking a break.

"Grace," Millie was at her side again, "there's a boy here, says he's from Granite Falls." Millie pointed toward a row of cots on the far end of the post-op tent.

"Really?" Grace's heart hammered, and her mind immediately went to Matthew.

"Not your brother," Millie said. Millie must have seen the hope and fear that had sprung to Grace's face. "Name's Jimmy Padgett, a young guy."

Grace looked in the direction of the cots again. Millie turned, walking in front of Grace down the line of cots.

"Nurse, I need a glass of milk," one soldier said from Millie's right. Millie was voluptuous and flirted with the soldiers to no end. Grace always smiled at these sorts of displays. They were harmless, and Grace thought they probably helped the soldiers get better. Helped them look more chipper, kept their health up for the pretty nurse Millie. Millie turned toward the soldier and put her hands on both shapely hips.

All the nurses wore men's uniforms, including the pants, and Millie's hips looked particularly curvy in Army pants.

"It sounds to me like you might be well enough to be moved back to the evacuation hospital."

The soldier smiled and put up his hand, which was wrapped in white gauze bandages. Grace could see the same bandages around his ribcage and chest as well.

"No, no," The soldier gave a fake cough. "See, I'm not well enough. It's better if I stay here with you to keep an eye on me."

Millie shook her head with a wide grin on her face and then turned back to her path.

"Here he is," Millie gestured to a cot with a short, thin boy lying on it. He was missing both legs below the knees, had bandaging

14

around his head and neck, and Grace suspected he was probably barely awake. He would have been heavily anesthetized for surgery, and he would have a good amount of pain medication after that.

"Jimmy Padgett, this is Grace Finley. She's from Granite Falls too," Millie gave her little introduction, then raised her eyebrows at Grace and walked away up the tent, ignoring another comment from the other soldier as she walked by.

Grace looked at the boy carefully. She didn't think she recognized him, but she couldn't be sure with all the gauze covering his features.

"Hi Jimmy," Grace came around to the side of his cot. She knelt right on the ground next to him. "A Granite Falls boy, are you?"

"Grace Finley," The boy said slowly. "Your mom is Ethel Finley?"

Grace's palms began to sweat, and her heart rate picked up. She was in the middle of France where millions of American boys and men were fighting and dying for their country. The chances of her meeting someone who knew her mother, came from the same town she was born and raised in, where only 5,000 people lived, were practically non-existent.

"You know my mother?" Grace spoke slowly. An image of her mother in her favorite blue housedress came to Grace, and she felt a knot rise in her throat.

"My mother is Trudy Padgett," the boy said, but this meant nothing to Grace. "My mother and your mother are both in the Blue Star Mothers of America Club. They meet at your house once a week."

Grace laughed. Before she left for Europe, she'd been doing her nursing courses and hadn't been home to be a part of her mother's meetings or social life. She remembered her mother saying something about it in a letter, but nothing more.

"I had no idea they met," Grace smiled.

"They make food and help the mothers with gold stars."

A gold star meant the mother had lost a child in the war, while a blue star meant their child was in the war, but was alive.

Now Grace understood. She could easily see her mother taking on all of the bereaved women in her town. She would make them dinners, help with housework, go and sit and listen to stories of the poor children who were now dead. It was just like her mother.

"With you here, I feel like I'm home. Do you?" Jimmy's one brown eye was open for Grace to see.

"Yes," She patted Jimmy's hand. "You'll be going home soon," Grace said. With no legs, he would arrive back in Granite Falls a young hero of the war, probably one of only a few young men to be back home at all. "From here, you'll go to an evacuation hospital, then to a general hospital, and then you'll get on a hospital ship bound for home. They will throw you a parade."

The young man smiled weakly at the thought of a parade.

"The high school marching band will play for you, and everyone will visit you. You'll be a celebrity." Grace wanted to keep the smile on his face.

Jimmy looked at her with his one free eye, and Grace patted his hand again.

"You should get some rest now," Grace stood.

"You'll come back?" Jimmy's question was plaintive and scared, and the sound of his voice made Grace sad.

"Of course! When you wake up, I'll be here." Grace looked down on him and felt like she also was his mother. She wondered if he'd lied about his age and enlisted early. "Get some sleep now."

Jimmy's eye followed her around the cot where she gave one more smile before walking toward the other side of the tent. On the other side, there were other patients to check on, give medications to, and change dressings for.

Grace worked into the afternoon of the next day. The adrenaline had pushed her through, but she was exhausted. Her fingers were sore and raw, her mind fuzzy, and her feet numb.

"Eileen says I'm to send you to go get some sleep." Mae, one of the other nurses, took the fresh dressing out of Grace's hand. "Go, I'm good here."

Grace let the gauze and wrapping be taken from her hands.

"Thank you, I feel like I could fall asleep standing up right here."

"I'm not sure your cot will be much better," Mae said with a bite. Mae was always complaining about something. Grace knew that the other woman didn't mean anything by it, but she did wish Mae would just keep it to herself sometimes.

"I'm going to check on one person before I leave," Grace turned and walked in the opposite direction from the tent where she would sleep. She walked backed toward Jimmy Padgett's cot, remembering her promise to him.

As soon as Grace's eyes settled on the young boy, Grace knew something was wrong.

"Jimmy?" Grace said softly, so as not to awaken the other soldiers sleeping nearby. Jimmy's face was tight, and his body was shaking. Grace checked his pulse and opened his one free eye.

"Mae, we need a doctor. Something's wrong," Grace called over to the other nurse. Mae looked at the cot Grace was sitting next to, then ran out of the tent in search of a doctor.

"Jimmy, everything's okay, you've come through the hardest bit, and you'll come through this too." Grace was certain that he couldn't hear her, but she spoke to him anyway. "Jimmy, I want you to think of your mother, think of Granite Falls. Can you remember the smell of the ground after the rain? Do you remember the fair in the springtime and all the animals that would come in from the farms? You need to think about home, Jimmy.

18

You're on your way there now, you'll be home just in time for your very own parade—you don't want to miss that, do you?" Grace could hear the panic rising in her voice. "Jimmy?"

Jimmy's body had seized up, his back was lifted off the cot, his head and the stumps of his legs pressing down. His jaw was clenched, and it looked like foam was creeping down the side of his face, seeping out of his tightly closed lips.

"Jimmy!" Grace looked over his body and felt tears spring to her eyes. She'd cried every day since she'd started as a nurse. Seeing men wounded in this way, men die in front of her eyes, men who were scared of death, men who had already seen their friends die on the battlefield...none of it ever got easier for her.

"Lord," Grace whispered, "please protect Jimmy. If it is your will to take him, then let him go without fear, with a calm mind, with a loving heart, let him go with you, Lord. Let Jimmy walk with you."

Jimmy's body fell back into the cot, unmoving. Grace felt the hot tears coursing freely down her cheeks. She'd managed to keep her crying to her cot. She'd made a promise to herself that she wouldn't let the other soldiers see her cry, that she would smile for them, be strong for them, have hope for them. But not today. There was something about the young man. His youth, the excitement she'd seen in his eyes over going home, of having a parade in his honor. The thought of his mother sitting next to hers. Whatever it was, it felt so deeply personal.

Grace's hands shook as she reached her fingers to his neck wrist and felt for a pulse.

"What's happened?" Eileen's voice was behind her. The doctors must have all been busy. Eileen lifted his wrist as well. Her eyes moved to Grace's.

"He had some sort of fit, epileptic or something else. He seized up." Grace pushed the tears off of her cheeks.

Eileen nodded and exhaled as she put Jimmy's hand back on the cot, "He's gone now." Grace looked at the body of the boy and was thankful that since she could not be strong, that someone else could be.

Chapter Three

O'Brien walked the three soldiers up to the front. There were foxholes for the soldiers, who were now seated low into the earth.

"I'm going to create cover for you here. We have our troops moved in further east. Once you get just south of here, we'll get you in there. That way you'll have the cover of the forest to help you stay unseen by German eyes." O'Brien walked the three further south until they could move east into the forest that was acting as the new battle ground. "Ok, Matthew, find your coordinates now so you know exactly where you're starting from." Matthew pulled out his compass and his map.

"How will I see to mark the map in the dark?" Matthew looked down at the map and could barely see anything on it. They were under the light of the moon, but soon every bit of moonlight would be obscured by trees.

"Do your best, wait for moonlight, remember what you can," O'Brien's face didn't look very hopeful, and Matthew felt the futility of their mission even more. If this was the most important part, knowing where the Germans and their weapons were, then as much as the darkness would act as a safeguard for them, it would also act as a hindrance. As dark as it was, they could walk right into a German soldier and not realize it.

"Some of the German soldiers may be equipped with a new technology that helps them see in the dark. We don't think many have it, and we think it's unlikely that you'll be at much of a disadvantage, or we wouldn't be sending you." O'Brien seemed torn on telling them this bad news.

Matthew's heart sank. The reality was that O'Brien was telling them, which meant it was very possible that the Germans would be at the full advantage.

"Your main advantage is that they don't know you're there. Try to keep it that way." O'Brien swallowed then took a breath, "Ok, we're ready. You stay here. I'll move north and get some guys to fire as a distraction. When you hear the artillery, that's your cue to move. Got it?"

Matthew nodded and looked to the two men standing next to him.

They all huddled next to a grouping of trees. There were other American soldiers near them, but soon that wouldn't be the case.

Matthew's ears were waiting for the sound of fire, the hairs on his arms standing on end. He looked into the darkness, trying to see if anyone lay in wait for them. He couldn't tell. They had no idea if German soldiers were twenty feet or a thousand feet away. They would just have to have faith that in the dark of the night the Germans wouldn't want to be too close to the Americans. Matthew was betting on at least two hundred feet of soldier-free territory.

"We'll follow your lead," William whispered, and Tony nodded his agreement. Matthew felt a heaviness fall down on his chest. He didn't want to be responsible for the lives of William and Tony. He had no special knowledge that they did not have, only the idea of the direction they would be facing and roughly where they were in the world. The Germans had occupied this territory only weeks ago. They could have hidden traps and explosives anywhere they wanted to. Despite the cold, Matthew felt a drip of sweat trailing down the back of his neck, moving coolly down his spine.

"It shouldn't be long now," Tony said.

The anticipation was almost worse than the movement itself. Matthew braced himself. Just as O'Brien had said it would, the guns started firing in the distance. Matthew's ears pricked up. He would have to listen for movement as much as he would have to look for it. Matthew got low and began moving forward from tree to tree. He continued on until he heard the guns begin to slow down. In his mind, he estimated that they had run a hundred and fifty feet. The three men stood with their backs to trees as they tried to recover their breath.

"What are we going to do now?" William whispered as quietly as he could.

"We move silently," Matthew whispered, pointing. He gave them all time to catch their breath and for their eyes to adjust as much as possible to the darkness that surrounded them.

There were no sounds thus far. If they were close to the Germans, then the Germans weren't making any noise either. Matthew tapped William on the shoulder and motioned his movements. If he went due north, then they should be very close to the German lines. As quietly as possible, Matthew stepped over leaves and sticks. Every twenty-five to fifty feet, they stopped to let the silence absorb any sounds they might be making. They

23

listened for signs of Germans, watched the darkness for them, but they saw and heard nothing. It was possible that they were much further from them than they thought. Perhaps the Germans did not like fighting in the forest—except that they had been holding off the Americans so well.

Matthew continued north, and William and Tony followed. It was not an easy journey with them all knowing that at any moment and without any warning they could all be killed. Matthew had to rely on his ears and sense of placement more than his eyes. He could step right into a trap, into a ditch, into a den full of Germans, and he wouldn't even have time to prepare for it.

Suddenly, Matthew stopped.

Neither of his companions made a noise or asked a question, they could feel that Matthew was listening, and so they too listened.

There was a sound that Matthew didn't recognize—it was possibly an animal or something unrelated to the war, but Matthew didn't think so. He pulled his weapon from its holster, getting ready to shoot if he needed to.

The noise stopped and still the three soldiers waited. Nothing happened. It was a full thirty minutes before Matthew moved again. He walked to the side of the tree they were standing around and looked for a sign of movement.

Peering into the darkness, he saw nothing. Then far off, he saw a little red glow. A soldier was smoking a cigarette. Matthew assumed the glow to be at least two hundred feet from where they stood. They would have to move closer if they were to get the information that O'Brien and the Colonel wanted from them.

Matthew tapped the two men on the shoulder and began moving east, further into the forest. Everything slowed down into a painful drag forward. There were too many risks to moving quickly, so they moved a hundred feet east as slowly as possible. Now at a hundred feet away from where the glow had been, they stopped. Matthew got low to the ground and looked for any other red dots in the darkness. Anything that might give away a human presence.

Matthew marked the location mentally, then motioned the other two men that they should head further north. After another hour, they found signs of life. Matthew's adrenaline had never pumped so hard in his life, and he was able to do absolutely nothing about it but to remain silent.

As they sat and listened, Matthew looked at William to see if the other man was making any sense of what he was hearing. William seemed to be concentrating, but when he caught Matthew's eye, he shook his head. Matthew understood that he was getting nothing good. They headed slowly on, looking for the next spot where they might find Germans talking or where they might be able to see weapons.

It took over an hour for them to move north in the forest. They spotted a few more soldiers, but they didn't appear to be in large enough groups to be guarding anything. Each time, the three men hunkered down for William to listen to the men speaking. On their next stop, they seemed further away from the Germans than they had been, and Matthew wondered if the line went further east and if they would have to move. Matthew went to the ground behind another cluster of trees. He crouched close to the other two men.

"I think they must be farther east. We should have seen more of them by now."

"Unless they're asleep on the job," Tony said.

"Maybe," Matthew nodded slowly. "Or they could be just over that little hill?"

"They weren't saying anything useful," William shook his head.

"Ok," Matthew nodded. "I'm going to use that patch of moonlight to mark what we've seen, then we'll press east? Are you ok with that?"

William and Tony both nodded thoughtfully. Matthew moved a few feet until his hands were in moonlight. He pulled out his map and pencil and began making notations about what they'd seen thus far. Looking at it again, he thought the little hill would be a good place for the Germans to store weapons. They could dig into the hill and keep them out of eyesight. He circled the spot on the map.

Matthew moved back to the other two men. "We'll break for ten minutes, and then move east." He leaned back against the tree and exhaled slowly. For the first time since they'd been out in the forest, Matthew felt at peace. He encouraged his heart into a normal pattern and tried to breathe at regular intervals.

"Matthew," William's voice was in Matthew's left ear. "Have you always believed in God?"

Matthew turned to look at the man on his left.

"Yes, always." Matthew whispered back.

"But, how can you be sure?"

Matthew could practically hear William's mind moving. "I just am. He's always been by my side, no matter what. More than any person, more than anything, God has been present. All I had to do was ask, and He's always been there."

William was silent, and the sounds of the forest began to lift to Matthew's ears. The night animals and insects were coming out and would help cover any noise the three men might make. It would help.

"Ask what?" William's voice came to Matthew from the quiet. Matthew smiled.

"Ask for Jesus to be my savior." *Guide my words*, Matthew prayed in his mind. "For him to guide me, to be with me, to never leave my side."

Matthew watched William nod, and then the silence engulfed them again.

"We should move," Matthew said when he knew William was done asking questions. The two men nodded, and Matthew turned back to the small hill.

Chapter Four

William's mind had been working with a sharpness unknown to him since they'd entered the forest. He knew a vague sort of German from his grandmother who had been a German immigrant. His grandmother was still alive and felt so guilty for her heritage now that she had turned into more of an American patriot than anyone else their town.

William's grandmother had always lived with their family, and William had picked up some of the German she spoke almost exclusively. During the Great Depression, William's father had lost his job and killed himself. William was only a kid when it happened, but he got a job, and eventually his mother got a job as well. They all moved to a smaller house in a poor neighborhood, but during those times, people didn't look down on the poor. Everyone was poor. Everyone was having a hard time. The only thing that mattered was keeping their family alive.

There was never a question of William going on to college. There was no money for college, and William would never have asked his mother for it if there had been. He'd graduated up the ladder at the pharmacy where he'd worked at as a boy. He would have stayed there if the war hadn't come.

Now, he was deep in a German forest, trying to understand a thick fluent German that was nearly impossible to hear. He had found himself bracing for death when they'd all first dropped down in Normandy, but at some point, he simply couldn't brace himself anymore. He gave himself over to fate. If he were meant to die, then he would; if he weren't, then he would go home when this was all over.

Matthew had come with him as a welcomed friend. Watching Matthew, William felt like he was learning a lot. William hadn't been able to spend a lot of time with other men. He hadn't had a father or brother in the house, so he only had an idea of what other men were really like. His idea was all wrong when it came to Matthew though. Matthew had a way of listening. He seemed incredibly wise for a person so young, and he naturally acquired the respect of all those around him.

Right now, Matthew was slowly and steadily leading them to the hill, now only fifty feet in front of them. William was almost certain there was something horrible waiting on the other side, but there were no sounds from there, and they'd had no evidence of a person for the last hour. It would begin to get light soon, and they would have nothing to take back to the Army at all. Matthew put up a hand and stopped both William and Tony.

"You both stay here and train your guns on the hill in case I need help."

"I'm not letting you go up there alone," William said. "Tony is the sniper, he can hold cover for both of us."

Matthew looked at William for a long moment.

"There's no point in our both getting killed if it isn't safe."

"—and if it isn't safe, then you'll need my help to get out alive." William could not let Matthew go alone. It was against his grain. If they were set to die, then they would die together.

Matthew nodded and motioned Tony to take cover. Tony did, and Matthew and William both trained their guns in front of them. Matthew moved forward just as silently as he had been doing all night. William stayed at his side, moving with just as much control and just as noiselessly.

There was a stretch of hill leading to the top where no trees grew and which would leave them exposed until they made it to the other side. The men both got low to the ground, trying to stay as invisible as they could. As they reached the top of the mound, William saw another red dot like the one they'd seen before. He put a hand out to stop Matthew.

A German officer was smoking only feet from where they lay. There was a dim light and another officer maybe twenty feet off from the first.

Immediately William's body began to react. His chest inflated with air, and his breathing took on a shallow quality that made him feel as if he weren't getting enough oxygen.

"Ich bin hungrig . Haben Sie etwas zu essen ?" The solider talking was young, younger than either William or Matthew. He was just complaining about being hungry and asking for food.

"Nein. Bleibst du hier? Ich muss pissen." The taller soldier walked off toward the trees furthest from the men to empty his bladder. William knew that if a soldier had to be there at all times that there was something special to protect. His hands were sweating, and he was afraid that if he had to raise his rifle it would slip right out of his hands.

William had just begun to think that the two of them could easily take both the young soldier out and the other soldier releasing his bladder into the trees, when a sound made his stomach turn. A group of three soldiers was walking toward the young soldier.

"Alles in Ordnung?" One soldier, the oldest looking, asked if everything was all right while walking right up to the hill. The soldier leaned close and picked up a machine gun. Matthew had been right to come up here, they had at least found one stash of weaponry.

William was ready to begin his retreat back down when he heard a click at his head.

He didn't have to turn around to know what was happening. Behind him right now was a rifle, trained on his head. He could practically feel the breath of it on his neck just beneath his helmet.

"Nicht bewegen!" The soldier yelled for them not to move. The other soldiers looked up to where they lay.

A crisp shot echoed into the night, and there was a thud behind them as blood splattered the back of their bodies. William got up and grabbed Matthew whose body was partially underneath the now dead soldier.

Tony had taken the shot. Immediately there was another shot from one of the German soldiers. William lifted his rifle and began shooting as he backed down the hill. When he was part way down, he turned and began running.

There were shouts behind him from the Germans. Matthew was still at his side.

"Go!" Matthew yelled to Tony, who had his rifled raised still ready to cover them as the Germans moved forward. Two shots rang out from Tony, and then a third. The last was not Tony's bullet, and it made contact with Tony's head. The sound of impact rang in William's ears only feet from where he stood.

William looked at Tony's disfigured face as he crashed face first into the soil.

"Let's go!" Matthew yelled in his ear, pulling him to the cover of the trees. Matthew pulled William in front of himself and yelled at him. "Run!"

The two men took off back toward US lines. William knew, just as Matthew must, that they had to go back to US-controlled territory carefully. If they came running like this, then they were likely to be shot by their own men thinking they were Germans.

"Gehen!" William heard one soldier yell to another soldier behind them.

William's head was spinning. They should move south again, lose the soldiers, and then return to their own side.

"Left!" Matthew tried to yell under his breath so as not to tip off the Germans of the direction they were going.

The two men ran with a speed that left all their careful slow steps hanging painfully in the past. Running at this pace, they would reach the southern entrance they'd used coming in, much faster than it had taken them to get as far north as they had.

They kept running until Matthew pulled on William's arm. Slowed him to a halt and walked him silently to a large jutting tree.

"This is where we stopped when we came in," Matthew whispered. "If we go straight west, we should find our camp. We need to go slowly, though."

William nodded. He was breathing so heavily that he was sure everyone on both sides of the forest could hear him.

"We'll take a minute to catch our breath." Matthew turned his head to listen for the Germans. They'd heard them through their run, but only silence met their ears now. "I don't know where they are. I thought they were just behind us, but now I don't hear anything."

William tried to stop his labored breathing so he could hear more clearly, but he couldn't. He had to control his impulse to stand up and run the rest of the way back to their base. No American guards really knew they were out here. Maybe their fellow soldiers wouldn't shoot, but they probably would. They wouldn't know to watch for two American soldiers on the other side of the American line.

They sat silently for long minutes without a sound from the Germans. Finally, William's breath came back down from where it had been, and Matthew finished marking his map in code. That way, if they both ended up shot and the Americans found their bodies, their Captain would have a working map. If they were shot, but the Germans found their bodies, the Germans wouldn't understand what the Americans were after, though it wouldn't be all that difficult for them to guess.

The two sat for another ten minutes without a sound being heard, then Matthew leaned close to William.

"Can I ask something of you?" Matthew's eyebrows were drawing in toward each other, and William could now see the sweat that ran across his forehead.

"Of course," William said back.

"I have this feeling," He shook his head trying to take back his words and restart what he was trying to say. "If something happens to me here tonight, I want you to visit my family when you get home."

"Nothing will happen to you," William was scared for Matthew's words. They sounded knowing in a way that William didn't like. "We are close to our side, we'll be out in an hour."

"The sun is about to come up," Matthew said as if this were supposed to explain something.

"Nothing is going to happen," William said again. Matthew turned to him and said, "If it does, then I am ready to go. You don't have to worry about that."

35

William opened his mouth to say something else, but Matthew put his hand up in a way that made William close his mouth again.

"Promise me that you will go to see my family. That is all I want. You don't have to tell them anything about tonight. I just want you to tell them that I died at peace. That I wasn't afraid, that they can mourn my loss but that they should not mourn my death." Matthew waited, looking William in the eye.

William could not refuse the man in front of him. If it would make him feel better to hear William say it, then William would not keep that from him.

"Of course, I will do that, but you are not going to die, so I will not have to keep my promise."

"One day we will all die," Matthew said, closing his eyes and leaning his head back on the tree behind him. He looked more at peace now that William had promised, though the promise hadn't made William feel any more at peace.

"Then, will you do the same, if I die tonight and you live? Will you promise to visit my family?" William waited, watching the outline of Matthew's face.

Matthew turned his head to William, "I promise that nothing will happen to you tonight."

Chapter Five

Grace slept for the rest of the day. She didn't wake until it was dark outside.

The sound of "I Had the Craziest Dream" by Harry James and his Orchestra played in her half-waking, half-sleeping thoughts. One of the girls had brought a record player along with them, and since she only had room for a few records, Grace had become intimately familiar with the songs on each one.

Harry James and His Orchestra, Glenn Miller, Tommy Dorsey, and Bing Crosby were the musical guests that played the background music to every stop they made. Grace had decided that she would marry Bing Crosby if he weren't already married. Just to hear him sing to her everyday would be a perfect world. She was certain that his voice was what heaven would be like.

Grace opened her eyes and stared at the Army green canvas in front of her face. She breathed slowly as she let the events of the night and morning before she'd fallen asleep sink back into her consciousness. She remembered the sight of Jimmy's face, what she could see of it, before she'd left him to rest. When he'd looked like he was just about to fall asleep like any other soldier who might fall asleep and wake up feeling slightly better or worse.

When the song was over and the next one began, Grace turned over. "I've Heard That Song Before," was coming on. Grace sat up and smiled at the other girls in the tent: Mae, Millie, Ruby, and Alice. Millie and Alice were dancing with each other,

Mae was swaying to the sound of the music, and Ruby was rolling her hair.

Millie twirled Alice and led her into a dip. Alice squealed and fell over. Grace couldn't help but laugh along with them. Grace breathed in a deep breath and let all thoughts of Jimmy flow out of her mind. There would be plenty of time to mourn on her own and with others, but not tonight. For a few minutes, she wanted to forget that she was in a field hospital in France.

Alice was making her way back to her feet. She ignored Millie's offer to dance again and went instead to Mae. Mae stood up and began dancing with Alice, so Millie turned to Grace and held out her hands to her.

Grace shook her head, "No, no."

Millie grabbed her arms anyway.

Obliging her friend, Grace stood and began a cramped dance in the middle of their tent. Ruby clapped her hands once she'd secured her last twist of hair.

"Please have them play it again, and I'll remember just when..." Millie sang and Grace hummed along. Millie twirled Grace, and Grace laughed again.

The song ended, and Millie gave Grace a little bow to which Grace curtseyed. She sat back on her cot with a flop, and Millie sat next to her. "Sleepy Lagoon" started, and Millie began rocking her head back and forth.

"Have you slept at all?" Grace looked at Millie. Millie looked as fresh as if she'd slept a full ten hours sleep.

"Not yet," Millie smiled and lifted her eyebrows. "I'm going to sleep any minute now."

Grace tilted her head down and looked at her friend over her eyes.

Mae sat down where she'd been before, and Alice moved to her own cot where she had a helmet full of water. It looked as though Millie had forced Alice from her task of washing out her "delicates" to dance. Alice dunked her underthings a few times and then walked her helmet and her wash out of the tent to dump the water from her helmet and ring out her silky unmentionables.

She came back in carrying both. She hung her silky little shorts and her brassiere at the end of her cot, then lay back looking at the ceiling of green canvas. Her knees now moved gently to the flow of the slower song.

Alice turned and pulled an envelope out from under her pillow. The envelope had already been opened, and she was obviously rereading its contents. Grace watched Alice with envy. She'd been waiting for a letter from her brother for three weeks, and she'd heard nothing.

"How is Barry?" Grace asked. Barry was Alice's fiancé. He was posted back home because of his advanced engineering background. He was working on things for the government that he couldn't even tell Alice about. The girls liked to come up with theories when they talked about Barry's work. Making bombs,

39

creating some new sort of weapon the world hadn't seen before, creating a machine that could fight by itself without the need of American boys. The possibilities were endless, but the reality was probably much more boring than their guesses.

"He's talking about all the women working in factories back home." Alice turned over onto her stomach and looked at Grace. "Can you imagine? All of the jobs men used to do, and now women are building things?"

"Perhaps it isn't so different from nursing? We do things we never thought we'd do. We've seen war. We jumped in the water at Normandy only days after the boys were on the ground."

Alice stared at the ground, then looked back at Grace, "Yeah, I guess. Sometimes I wish I'd just moved into a factory job instead of coming out here. Then at least I could be with Barry."

"But you're a great nurse! Think of all the lives you've saved already." Grace didn't want to admit that the sound of being at home was very appealing. It was hard living out here. They had to pack up the entire field hospital every eight to eleven days and move it along with the soldiers. They had to dig and put up tents and cots and set up I.V.s. Then just when that was done, a barrage of bloody, broken soldiers would come in. That's when the real work began. It was overwhelming. Grace knew that the things she saw everyday out here would stay with her for the rest of her life.

"Did you see your mail?" Alice pointed to the foot of Grace's cot. Grace looked down, and her heart bounced. She hadn't thought that Alice was reading a new letter. The mail must have come in while Grace was sleeping.

Eileen walked into the tent with force, "Ok, ladies, I need two extra hands." She looked at the girls sitting in the tent. All of the girls looked away. They'd all had a long night. "I take it I don't have any volunteers?"

Grace leaned over and picked up the two separate envelopes addressed to her.

"I'll come," Grace said still not looking up. "If I can just have a few minutes to read my mail?" She looked up at Eileen. Eileen looked down at the two letters in Grace's hands. Eileen's face changed, and she looked back to Grace.

"I'll go," Alice said. Suddenly sitting up, Alice's eyes were on Grace's hands too. Grace looked back to the envelopes. The one now on the bottom was in her brother's handwriting, the other one on top was typed out.

"You stay here, you had a long shift." Eileen said uncomfortably. Grace knew that everyone had had a long shift. It wasn't a good excuse.

"That's ok," Grace was getting scared, she felt her hands shaking, and something in brain was refusing to work. "I don't mind." She stood, grabbing for her trousers.

"Grace," Eileen put a hand on Grace's shoulder. "You had better stay here and read your mail." Grace could feel her throat closing off, and she thought she might just stop breathing.

"Please," Grace said looking at Eileen. She wasn't pleading to work. She was pleading for Eileen to say that Grace could read her mail after she'd worked another shift—that it would be waiting for her later—that nothing from back home was that important, like she often did when one of the girls was dying to read her correspondence. But Eileen didn't say that. She didn't say Grace's mail was trivial because Eileen, as well as everyone else in the tent, knew that Grace's mail wasn't trivial. It was something else entirely.

"I'll come," Mae stood looking at Grace with the same fear that Grace felt.

"I need to borrow something," Ruby gestured out of the tent, then left. Eileen waited for Mae and Alice to leave the tent, then put a hand on Grace's shoulder. Squeezed it, then left.

Millie stood across from Grace, "Do you want me to stay?"

Grace shook her head.

"I'll be outside if you need me," Millie's face was pinched as she left. The music was still playing, a light airy tune.

Grace brushed her fingers across the top envelope and placed it next to her. She picked up her brother's envelope and kissed it. Then, she flipped it over and pushed her thumb under the flap, gently ripping the paper back.

The paper was cleaner than it should have been. Grace could imagine her brother taking pains to keep it from the dirt around him.

September 26th, 1944

My Dear Sister Grace—

As I write this letter I am imagining your face, just as you looked the last time I saw you. Occasionally, I see a nurse in my travels that reminds me of you, and I wonder what you're doing. Are you scared? When it becomes too much, do you turn your cares over to God? Every day when I open my eyes, my first prayers are for you and our parents. We've both made it this far, and for me at least, it's been one heck of a journey.

I've felt God's presence follow me through every foxhole, each ditch, and no matter what was going on around me, I've never felt alone. I've been getting a peculiar feeling that started a few minutes ago. I'm going on a special mission with two other men. One of them, a guy named William from Thief River Falls, Minnesota. Can you imagine a guy all the way from Minnesota becoming a true friend of guy from North Carolina? It becomes a very small world out here on the battlefield.

This feeling I have… I feel like God is telling me something. Telling me that I may not make it back from this one. I don't know why, but I can only trust in God's plan for me. I trust in his plan for you too, little sister. I'm so proud of you. You are so brave and kind, a woman of honor and integrity. You are a woman of God, and for that I am truly grateful because I know I won't have to worry about you. God will take care of you if I am gone.

Please, don't be sad for me. I am fulfilling God's purpose for my life as I always hoped to do. I love you dearly and am only sad that I won't be able to say goodbye to you and our parents in person.

I love you, my dear Grace.

Your brother,

Matthew

Grace felt tears falling off her face, but she moved the letter so they wouldn't fall on the paper. The paper felt so fragile under her fingers, as if it could disintegrate at any moment. Grace reread each word.

"I love you, Matthew," Grace whispered to the paper before folding it gently and tucking it back into its envelope. Grace held the letter that her brother had held so recently, but she couldn't feel her brother in it.

With reverence, she set the letter down next to the other typewritten one.

Grace let her eyes rove over the plain envelope. Her name looked so impersonal, staring up at her from the front of it. Her mind felt sluggish, and her name suddenly blurred until she couldn't read it anymore. When one heavy tear dropped from her eye, her vision cleared again.

Grace picked up the thin rectangle with shaking hands. She inhaled slowly and then exhaled through her mouth.

"Please, don't take him from me. Please."

Chapter Six

William's stomach was beginning to twist. All he could think of was getting himself and Matthew back to their side of the fighting line.

"Are you ready to go?" Matthew asked, turning his head once more.

William nodded, though he could barely imagine his body moving. Despite his reluctance, William stood as Matthew stood. The two men peered into the dark. They could see no one, hear no one. William pulled his pistol out, feeling that he had a better chance of handling the smaller weapon then the larger one.

"Let's move one tree over," Matthew whispered so quietly that William could barely hear him. William nodded, and followed Matthew's lead slowly and silently to the next grouping of trees. Matthew held up a finger to indicate that they would be moving one more time.

This time William had more confidence. They'd moved once already, and this was just a repeat of their previous action. For the first time, Matthew gestured for William to go first. A small fuzzy, prickling thought began to scratch at the back of William's mind, but he ignored the thought and moved as Matthew indicated.

To William's right came the same click he'd heard only an hour ago. From his peripheral vision he could see the shiny tip of gun mental in the moonlight. William spun around in place raising his gun as he went. Two shots cracked out at the same time. William saw in a blur the form of Matthew as he moved purposefully in front of William.

Two forms collapsed to the ground. There was a flurry of shots fired from both the American and German borders. William had to take cover at the base of the tree he had just been moving to. He sat with his back to the tree, his eyes focused on the ground in front of him. Discarding his gun, William moved forward on his hands and knees toward Matthew's body. He turned it over and saw the bullet hole lodged in his chest.

William moved his fingers to Matthew's neck, looking for a pulse. A small breath oozed out of his throat.

"Matthew?" William could barely speak. The sounds of the breath gave him hope, but as he watched for another, there was none. He felt again for a pulse and found nothing. "Hold on. Please, hold on."

The sun was coming up. For the first time in the forest, William could see what lay around him. He could see a young German soldier lying dead at the base of a different tree. He could see the shape and color of the leaves they'd stepped on as they'd walked untraced through the forest last night, back when they were three instead of one. He could see the red fluid that flowed out of the child soldier and into the ground beneath him. He could see birds flying from tree to tree, even though there would be gun fire here at any moment.

He took a cold breath in and exhaled into the space in front of him. His breath showed hot against the cold day. It felt appropriate that today should be so cold. It felt appropriate that people on both sides of the forest should be uncomfortable today.

For a brief moment, William wondered about the young German soldier's family. He certainly had a mother and father just as every human did. He might have siblings as well. As impractical as it felt, he might have a wife, even a child. Looking at his shape strewn out on the ground, William thought him to be too much of a child himself for that.

He remembered that he'd heard the soldier saying he was hungry. He'd wanted something to eat, but he'd never had the chance, and now the boy was lying face down on the forest floor with nothing in his belly but a bullet.

William turned around and pulled at Matthew's body. He lifted his body by the armpits and began dragging him backwards toward the American camp. When he came close enough to see movement, William moved behind a tree again for safety. He moved his face around the side of the tree, toward the soldier, and whistled loudly.

"I'm an American," William yelled. "I was sent over by my platoon leader, Tom O'Brien. My name is William Sawyer, and I am with my fallen friend, Matthew Finley, Jr." William pressed his head back against the tree, the bark cutting into the back of his head. He closed his eyes tight and waited for a response from the other side of the tree.

"Throw your weapons down." William heard an American voice saying back to him. He could hear the panic in the voice, the indecision about what to do. Right now the soldier was thinking that William might be a German, speaking perfect English. That he'd stolen the uniform from an American body, and that the fallen friend was really a very much alive soldier ready to jump up and shoot when they both got close enough.

William threw his rifle and handgun on the ground where the other soldiers could see it.

"Please just get my commanding officer," William yelled. He'd been waiting this long, he could wait a little longer.

William stayed where he was, with guns trained on the tree at his back, and the sun coming up in the sky above him, until Tom O'Brien himself had been found and brought to the front. William hadn't wanted to wait so long for fear of the Germans, but he also didn't want to be killed by his own men. To him, the thought of being killed by the home team would be far more unbearable. When William dragged Matthew's body with him all the way back to O'Brien, two soldiers came forward to take the body in.

"Wait," William bent down and took the map from Matthew's body. Then he crouched, looking at his friend's face for the last time. Silently he thanked Matthew for his own life, though he felt as though he didn't deserve it. Silently he felt the sharp edge of guilt wedge deeply between his ribs.

William stood slowly, his body shaking, feeling drained and hopeless. He watched the two soldiers walking Matthew's body away to the place they took all the bodies. Now Matthew would just be another body under a tarp, waiting to be taken back to US soil, waiting for more men to come in so there would be room for his body to go out.

He turned his attention back to O'Brien, took a short breath, and said, "Tony went down just in front of the German line," William said slowly. "Matthew made the map." He held the papers up in front of his face then handed them over to the senior officer.

"Are you ok?" O'Brien looked concerned as he stared at William. William wanted to scream at him to stop. Of course he wasn't ok, but he couldn't say as much. More than anything or anyone, it was Tony and Matthew who weren't ok. They would never be ok again.

William was taken back to the tent to lie down and get some sleep after he'd talked with O'Brien and Colonel Swenson. The most important information had been captured by Matthew, and Matthew was no longer alive to tell them about it. They read the map and conferred among themselves before sending William back to his tent.

William sat on his cot as other soldiers from his platoon stared at him. They had probably heard something of what had happened that morning while William was trying to get back across the American line. Wilbur was out of the tent, and William didn't have time for anyone or anything but the memories that were burning through his brain.

He didn't even think of the promise he'd made until he'd lain down to try and sleep for a few minutes. The promise of visiting Matthew's family was suddenly hot across William's mind just as he closed his eyes. He knew that trying to sleep was futile, but he'd hope to just close his eyes and wish the thoughts away. Instead he heard Matthew's voice again. He'd known, somehow he'd known. William had not known. William had really thought that they had lost the Germans. William had been convinced that they were close enough, that together they could make it.

William's eyes opened, and he sat up. He couldn't imagine visiting Matthew's family. Matthew had taken a bullet for him. Matthew had died because of him. To go visit his family, to introduce himself, was a terrifying prospect. William stood up from his cot and walked out of the tent. He walked the line of tents and ignored everything that was going on around him. He needed fresh air. He needed to think without the clutter of other people speaking.

He moved around the camp, looking at no one, watching and hearing nothing but what played naturally in his mind. When he got to the edge of camp, William sat down.

What was he supposed to do now? What did all of this mean? Perhaps it meant nothing, that the desire to give meaning to the meaningless was just a natural human calling to help William feel better. Or maybe, it meant more than he could fathom.

William looked up at the sky, his eyes moving across the ever-brightening color, dipping to the horizon, and landing on the trees. Matthew had looked peaceful staring at these very trees. When Wilbur saw Matthew's body, he had thought him so peaceful that he had asked William if Matthew had been praying.

Praying.

William hadn't grown up with religion like Matthew. He didn't know the Bible, he didn't know why or how Matthew had prayed like he was talking to a friend. Just before Matthew had died, he'd said that he was not scared to die. He had said to tell his parents that they could mourn his loss but not his death.

How did a person who was staring death right in the face ever become so brave? How did he ever find a spiritual home so potent and powerful that he could lay himself in it right up to his last hour? Perhaps even *especially* in his last hour?

William didn't care if anyone was around him, if he was overheard or looked at. He bowed his head and tried to clear his mind.

What would Matthew say if he were here? No, that didn't work.

William took a breath and struggled with his mind.

"Lord," he finally said. Even the one word felt awkward on his lips. "I—I haven't done this before, but I guess you know that."

William licked his lips and sat motionless for a long minute.

"I don't know about any of this. I don't know if I even believe in you. I'm not sure if you exist or not, if Matthew was right to leave his life in your hands or if it was just…Well, I guess what I'm trying to say is that I don't know much about you. I don't know much about anything. I don't really know who you are but… I think I want to find out." William took a breath and looked up to the sky. It hadn't changed. He looked to the trees, but they were still there just the same.

Was he being stupid? Running to something because he was afraid? Because he wanted Matthew to be right? He couldn't be sure.

William walked slowly back to the tents. He walked until he found his own tent, then went inside and sat down on his cot. Across from his own cot was Matthew's. William stared at it for a long time, stared at Matthew's pack, which was still sitting just where it had been when they'd arrived here the night before.

William looked at it for a long time. Then, almost as slowly as they'd moved in the forest, William stood up and moved over to Matthew's cot. He felt the canvas bag beneath his fingers. It felt just the same as his own pack. William opened the pack, knowing what he expected to find. Something he'd seen before many times.

William moved the lining from the top and pulled the opening wide. He put his hand into the side. Tucked there, he found what he was looking for. William pulled out Matthew's black Bible. He opened the first page.

Matthew Finley, Jr. His name was written on the front cover. He flipped the fragile pages over and saw pencil markings, notes… he saw question marks and exclamation points. He continued to move through it, and the notes and markings never stopped. Matthew had notated through the entire thing. All of this belonged to his lost friend. William took the Bible and pressed it between his hands. This, he thought, he would take this home to Matthew's parents. William walked back to his own pack and tucked the book inside.

He thought briefly about trying to lie back down. He hadn't slept or had any rest in fifty-three hours, and his practical mind told him that he should lie down. He should get some sleep now while he had the chance. But there was another niggling feeling that pulled at the back of his mind.

William stood up abruptly and walked out of the tent.

Chapter Seven

"Please, don't take him from me. Please." Grace's voice was filled with fear, doubt, anger, and tears. She hadn't even opened the letter yet. Her heart was pounding a response. She stared at the letter and tried to find God's presence within her, but she felt nothing. She felt totally alone in the room. Her prayers felt unheard.

"God?" She looked up to the green canvas over her head. "Please. I know you answer prayers. You answered Elijah's prayer. Can you not answer my prayer as well?" She felt desperation growing within her. "Have I not been strong and courageous, Lord? I have not been afraid. I haven't been discouraged. Are you not to be with me everywhere I go?"

She closed her eyes and pressed her fingers together over the letter, "Where are you now, Lord? If you are to be with me, then where are you now?"

Her eyes opened to the sight of her own typewritten name.

Grace Finley.

"I will do anything. Anything. Just don't take Matthew from me. Please."

Grace's eyes lifted and moved over the green canvas. She waited to feel something, to feel a response to her prayer, but she felt nothing, only the warm paper between her fingers.

She turned the envelope over and placed her thumb underneath the flap. With a dragging, ripping finger, she opened the envelope and pulled out the typewritten letter within. The paper was thin and slipped under her fingers.

Moving her finger along the edge, she lifted the first flap, forcing her eyes away from the letter until she flipped the bottom open as well. Grace stared at the tip of her fingers. Slowly her eyes moved to the top of the letter.

She began to shake her head. The blood draining from her face, the hope she'd held draining from her life. Grace took a thick inhale of breath, but all that entered her lungs was despair.

"Matthew," Her voice was weak and plaintive.

September, 27th, 1944

My dear Miss Finley:

It is with deepest regret that I must relate the news that your brother, Private First Class Matthew Finley, Jr., died in action on September 26th, 1944 in Germany.

Private Finley has been noted above all else for his bravery in his service to his country. During a special operation, Private Finley stepped in the way of a bullet aimed at a fellow soldier. Your brother will never be forgotten. He will live on in all of the men here who have heard of your brother's heroic tale. Matthew went with a bravery that will not go unacknowledged.

You should also know that your brother helped to secure valuable intelligence during his last mission. This intelligence has already resulted in the saved lives of many American soldiers.

I extend my sincerest sympathies to you and your family on behalf of all of us here and on behalf of the U.S. Army.

Very Sincerely,

Charles R. Swenson

C.R. Swenson

Colonel, U.S. Army

Grace stared at the page. She was pressing the page between her fingers so tightly that her fingertips had turned white. She swayed under the heavy words that Colonel Swenson had used.

Would her parents have received word of this already? Would they have received a telegram or post? Imagining her mother and father receiving the news of her brother's death knocked the air out of Grace's lungs. Her mother had dedicated herself to the parents of dead soldiers. She'd doubtless hoped that her good deeds would help secure her son safety. She thought that God could not bestow such sad tidings on a family who had done so much for others who had lost those they loved.

Grace's eyes moved along the floor, then to her fingers, then they jumped back to the page she was at risk of ripping in her iron grip.

Died in action. Grace read the words, then kept reading the words over and over again, unable to process their meaning. Grace stared at the words for a long time until they blurred into black lines, nothing more.

She looked around her. There was no one in the tent with her. There was nothing to say that what she was experiencing in the moment was even real. She said nothing, made no exclamation, no movement. She felt her mind blur just as the words on the page had.

Fluttering fragments of her brother kept lifting up through her mind.

He had taken a bullet for a fellow soldier. He was brave. He was a hero.

Grace threw the page on the ground.

"I don't care." Her voice was real, and it brought her back to the tent, to her cot, to the reality that she was now facing; the reality that rang false to her disbelieving brain.

"I don't care about another soldier. I don't care about his being brave. I want Matthew. My Matthew," She said his name, and a deluge of feelings swam over her.

"Don't worry, I'll protect you," Matthew had said on her first day of High School. She'd been needlessly scared. Matthew had walked her to school that day. He'd waited for her after her first class.

But Grace had been ok. When she'd recovered from her first momentary fears, she'd told her brother that she was fine. She had dismissed his protection. She'd made friends so easily, right away in her first class of the year. Now she wished she'd done it differently. Everything differently. If only she had needed him more. If she had needed his protection, then maybe he wouldn't have sacrificed himself for someone else. Maybe he would have thought about her, that she needed him, that he must live if only to protect Grace.

Matthew had been so quiet. He'd had only one close friend and no girlfriends until he was a freshman in college. What if they had switched places? What if she had been the shy one? Would he now be alive, ready to protect his little sister, prepared to stay in this world because of the absolute certainty that his little sister still needed him?

Her mind began to roll through absurdities. She began to think of ways to save him, to bring him back. For a moment she had an overwhelming sense that she could change what she'd just read, that if she needed Matthew enough, he would come back for her. That she could rewrite history—perhaps even that this history hadn't really happened at all.

He could have stayed in school, should have stayed in school, but had left with only a year to go. He'd wanted to enlist in the Army. He had felt called. That's what he'd said to his parents. He'd told them that he valued the education they'd let him have, but that he felt "called to go." She could have stopped him then. She could have had an accident, could have flung herself from the roof, and forced him to stay by her side until the war was over. Just like a stupid child, she'd thought herself and Matthew impervious to the dangers of the war. She'd said with a confidence that only now felt ridiculous that she understood the dangers, but that she trusted that God would take care of her brother. She had not understood. What she'd trusted was that God would never let something like this happen to her brother. She'd trusted that her faith made her brother safe. But now her brother was dead.

"Dead," She heard her voice say the word. It sounded strange on her lips. "Matthew," Her lips formed around his name again. Matthew didn't play football, but he could outrun the entire football team. He was fast and strong, and he knew it. He was supposed to be fast enough, strong enough to get himself away from danger.

Why had he had to slow himself down for someone else? He had always looked out for other people, always. Grace had always loved that about her brother. Until today.

Now, she wished that he had been different. That he had been selfish. That he had protected himself first and others second. She didn't care about the man he saved or the soldiers he saved on the field. She wanted her brother. Only her brother.

Millie came in, and Grace looked up. Millie looked down at the letter that lay face up on the dirt in the middle of their tent.

"Oh, Grace," Millie sat down next to her and took Grace in her arms. "I'm so sorry."

Grace, who had felt the world surreal and changeable, suddenly felt the permanence and solidity of it. Something deep within snapped.

"Millie," Grace turned to her friend. "He's dead. My Matthew is dead."

Tears flooded over feelings, and suddenly she could hold nothing back. She sobbed into Millie's shoulder. Heavy, deep, sloppy sobs. She sobbed for her brother's pale face, the tiny freckles that dotted his nose, his clear blue eyes. She sobbed for the scar that ran through his eyebrow, the one he'd gotten when he was thrown from his bike when he was eight. Grace had been the one to cry when she'd seen his face dripping in blood, not Matthew. Matthew had only wanted to comfort his little sister.

She sobbed for curls that sprang at the base of his hairline.

Grace felt her heart and stomach squeeze so tightly she could not breathe. She gasped for air until her voice cracked out of her throat in a cry that sounded far from human. Grace sobbed for the man Matthew would never get to be. For the children he wouldn't have. For the seat that he wouldn't fill at the Finley dinner table. For the casserole he wouldn't eat. For the old man she would never know—and for the hole he had left in her heart that would never be filled again.

The record ended. With a scratch the needle skimmed across the shiny black surface waiting to be put back on track.

Chapter Eight

William walked with a decided purpose until he was back in front of O'Brien's tent. He looked at the tent and wondered briefly if he was quite in his right mind. When an answer didn't come to him, he pushed the thought aside and moved forward. William lifted the edge of the Army green flap and waited.

"Who is it?" O'Brien asked when he saw the flap of the tent flutter open.

William moved his mouth to the opening in the flap, "William Sawyer, sir, requesting permission to enter."

"Of course, Sawyer, come in."

William walked in with a confidence that surprised even himself. He felt calm and at perfect ease with what he was about to do.

O'Brien looked at William with concern, perhaps unable to figure out what had changed in the man in last hour. "Not able to sleep?" He asked.

"No, sir," William answered truthfully. "And I don't think I will be able to any time soon. At least not this morning, sir."

"I can understand that, Sawyer, but I'm afraid you'll have to—fatigue will make you careless—it can put you and your fellow soldiers at risk. More than two days awake is too much when we have the space and time for you to sleep." He paused,

"Especially right now, you've been through a lot—too much in the last few hours."

"I understand that, sir," William nodded but kept his lips pressed together as he tried to find his words.

"Then what can I do for you, Sawyer? Sleeping aid? A trip to the medic? Whatever you need, you've got it."

"None of those things, sir. The thing is… sir, I understand your not wanting me on the field."

William said nothing for a moment, and O'Brien waited expectantly. "But?" He prompted his soldier.

"But I think I need to be, sir. Be on the field that is. I want to finish the mission."

O'Brien leaned back in his seat and put both of his hands over his face, "Go on, continue."

"My friend died today, sir, during a reconnaissance mission, but that mission will be worthless if we don't do something with the information. Two men will have lost their lives for nothing if we don't make it back to those weapons and bring them back over the American line… if we don't bring them back to our side then—well, what was the point?"

O' Brien stared at William, then pushed himself up and moved in front of William. He put a hand on William's shoulder.

"You've been through a lot in the past twenty-four hours, Sawyer."

"That's true sir, but I don't think it will affect my performance, sir." William tried to stand as straight as he could. He wanted to look alert, alive, ready to move.

"Walk with me," O'Brien led William to the flap of the tent and then out into the open air. "It's daylight now. It was dangerous last night, and it will be nearly impossible this morning. Whatever happens now will most certainly result in American blood being spilled."

William wasn't sure if O'Brien was trying to warn him or dissuade him. It seemed to William that a man willing to go into enemy territory, face possible and perhaps probable death, was to be considered an asset and used immediately.

With this in mind, William decided not to say anything in response to O'Brien's comment.

"I have put together a team from your platoon. I think forty men spit up into three separate groups should be able to sneak in, take on the Germans that they will find, bring back a good amount of the goods they find, and still have room for casualties."

Planning for casualties felt a bit too realistic for William's taste. He wasn't sure what was pushing him forward now, but he had the distinct feeling that he was meant to go on this mission.

"I don't think we need that many people, sir. With all due respect." William's words seemed to catch O'Brien's attention.

"And how many people do you think you need?"

William thought about this for a moment as he tried to imagine everything happening in his mind. He'd seen the setup, the hill, and the amount of space that the Germans would have had to tuck supplies away in. It wasn't all that large. There couldn't be so many guns that such a large team would be needed. The smaller the team, the more likely they could go undetected.

It did seem unlikely for them to go unnoticed after the night before. Surely, now that the Germans knew the Americans were checking out that particular horde of weapons, they would be on the lookout for them with extra vigilance.

"Eight," William said. "Six to carry, two to cover their movements with fire if need be. I think eight is the most we could use and get everyone in and out alive."

"Eight?" O'Brien looked at William with a strange, curious appraisal. "Are you feeling ok, Sawyer? Feeling normal?"

"Well, frankly, no, I don't think I'm feeling normal sir, but I have a feeling about this mission. I don't know about other missions or battles, but this one..." William tapped into the deep-rooted feeling of resolve, the feeling that seemed to come from another place beyond him.

"And what if the men can't carry all the weapons away?"

"We destroy anything we can't take. If we can't use it, then we won't let the enemy use it either."

O'Brien walked a short line forward, then turned around and walked back.

"I don't know why, but against my better judgement, I'm inclined to believe you."

William nodded, understanding perfectly what O'Brien was saying and understanding that it had very little to do with William himself.

"And, after everything you saw this morning, you really think you can come out of that forest alive?" O'Brien pointed toward the trees and William followed his gaze.

"Yes sir, I do."

O'Brien exhaled and looked William over again, "And why is that?"

"Because, sir, Matthew told me that I'm not going to die today. And after this morning, I believe him."

Chapter Nine

"The Oberkassel railway bridge is gone, sir." Wilbur Archer was out of breath with the news. All the men in the group, including William, looked to O'Brien, who nodded at Archer as his face tightened.

"We better keep moving forward," O'Brien said as he turned back into the wooded hills they were making their way through. They were on a reconnaissance patrol looking, with little success, for a way for the American troops to cross the Rhine River.

The group moved forward in silence.

Wright, Neiman, and Shulman were all in front of William as they walked. No one talked. The atmosphere had been getting increasingly bleak as American troops made their way to various bridges along the Rhine and watched as Germans detonated bombs, demolishing each bridge and cutting the Americans off just as they arrived. They had to move forward, but their opportunities were quickly and literally disappearing.

"We should be coming up on the Ludendorff Bridge, sir," Jim Wright said quietly. "It connects with the town of Remagen, sir." The group walked on, O'Brien beginning to pull them out of their immediate cover so that they could get a look at the river.

Wright looked at his map and frowned, then moved on ahead of the group. O'Brien levelled the group off, knowing Wright would get a look and bring back word. The men continued their pace forward. Time was running short.

There was a soft sudden whistle from Wright's direction, and everyone stopped. When Wright didn't appear, William began to move in the direction the other man had gone. William's heart hammered whenever anything happened, good or bad. His body would tense, and he would prepare himself to see a friend killed in front of his eyes. But, when he arrived, Wright was not standing in a booby trap but rather smiling a big gap-toothed grin.

"Don't flip your wigs, boys, but we've got ourselves a bridge." Wright lifted his binoculars and looked over the structure as William and the other men ran up to see what he was seeing.

As soon as O'Brien saw the structure for himself, he pulled out his large radio and began sending off information, signalling Wright for coordinates.

"Southeast of Cologne," O'Brien said. "There's traffic going across right now, moving on the other side. German soldiers ready on this side," He looked through his binoculars again and spoke. "The normal sort of thing, but by the looks of it, if we could take them right now, we might catch them by surprise."

By the time O'Brien was off the line with command, the group was ready to run down and try to take the bridge themselves, though they were only a small group and not large enough to hold an entire bridge on their own.

O'Brien turned to his men with a strain of enthusiasm he hadn't displayed yet that day. "Won't be long, we'll have company soon

70

enough," O'Brien's voice sounded like a soft chant. "They're maybe two hours off. We just have to hope the bridge holds till then."

William watched each man in his group shift, pace, twitch, walk, or sink into a glassy-eyed reverie. He saw a few muscles spasm and Neiman's hands shake.

The group waited impatiently for almost three hours, an hour past the time O'Brien had predicted. The air was tight with tension. Each soldier saw their chances decrease with every moment that passed. Every man expected to see or hear an explosion, hear the stone base of the steal railway bridge crack apart and fall into the water beneath it.

By the time the other Americans made it, each man was exhausted from sitting with so much unusable energy. Now, if things worked out the way they hoped, a full-scale attack would quickly and successfully ensue.

"You ready to take this thing?" O'Brien asked as he turned to William, who happened to be standing next to the senior man when the first signs of a new platoon showed.

"Yes sir, I believe I am," William smiled back. O'Brien lifted his eyebrows, then turned to the incoming men.

Their small reconnaissance team had found a spot where they wouldn't be seen by the Germans but could run straight down onto the bridge and into their waiting victims.

"Good spot, O'Brien." The small, wiry man who came up behind O'Brien slapped him on the back in a jocular way that seemed incongruent with the bridge-storming that was about to take place and the possible lives that would be lost.

There wasn't time, in the small man's opinion, to wait for everything and everyone to be in perfect position. It was time to move. If the US Army didn't acquire this bridge, which was almost certainly the last one remaining across the Rhine River, then the Germans would have a serious advantage, and the US would have to spend a considerably greater amount of time, money, and effort to gain the territory on the east bank.

William looked through a light drizzle that he barely felt, what with his heavy gear, uniform, and the natural covering from the trees. He looked down at the railroad bridge that stood sturdily below. The bridge was three hundred or four hundred yards long with two sets of railroad tracks.

A few shooters were placed within the wooded area at close enough range to shoot the German soldiers still standing on the west bank closest to the American troops. William's heart pounded.

Before he had time to really prepare himself for the move, there was a signal, and the first pops of rifle fire echoed into the air. William watched a German soldier fall, then another. Men were moving all around him, and soon William's feet were thudding downhill along with them.

He was running toward the bridge like a fish in a large school swimming downstream. He could see the surprise and panic shown in the movements of the German soldiers. To his right, the

Americans took a German machine gun. Then the first American soldiers stepped onto the bridge.

There was a loud, dissonant crack. The Germans were trying to blow up the bridge. William ducked low as German bullets went whizzing past his head, some finding their target in his compatriots. A man was shot in front of him, and a spray of blood splattered back onto William's face.

US soldiers were cutting wires that led to demolition charges, others throwing them and kicking them off the bridge.

Something skidded against the outside of William's helmet. He felt a pull and drag that propelled him onto the ground. He watched as his helmet lifted into the air in front of him then went rolling away. There was no way to go after it. The men of the platoon were stampeding forward, and William barely made it back to his feet without being stepped on or over.

He gave a last fleeting look in the direction of his helmet then ran bareheaded onto the bridge. The thudding of boots hitting the steel bridge rang in his ears, and the structure vibrated under him.

The soldier directly to his right and a few paces ahead took enemy fire. The man's body hit William, knocking him sideways. His head made sharp contact with metal, and he felt something in his head give way. His body doubled over the railing, and his vision blurred. There was a brief moment, a spark of pain, before a feeling of weightlessness came upon him. Then, as cold water slapped hard against his skin, everything went dark.

~

"Fried chicken," a male's voice full of the American South called out next to William's left ear. "With potatoes, biscuits, with a heap of gravy poured on top… Oh my! I would spend the rest of my life celibate if I could have just one meal like that."

William cracked his eyes open, and a sharp pain shot through the front of his head immediately.

"Dunkirk, do you ever talk about anything but food?" Another man's voice came from a different direction, but the pain in William's head was too acute for him to place it.

"I've been making lists in my head of all the things I'm going to eat when I get home," Dunkirk said with a lusty hunger.

"Did you say you were making those lists in your *head*? Because I could swear you were saying it all out loud." The other voice didn't laugh, but someone else did.

"If you had a bullet hole in your stomach and all you could eat was watered-down mush, all you would think about was food too."

William tried to open his eyes again. His head was still pounding, but he didn't close them right away this time.

"Hey," a voice said nearby. The voice didn't say anything else, but suddenly William could feel eyes on him.

His own vision was strange, though he was only looking at the top of an army green tent. William moved his fingers slowly across the rough cotton sheet his hand was lying on. He moved his neck to the side an inch, and another blast of pain lit up the front of his head.

"Nurse," one of the voices rang in his ears.

Every move, every twitch, every sound, pounded in his head. He felt like a deep sea diver at the point in the ocean where the force of water pushes so hard that it can crunch a tin can.

There were sounds all around him, but he tried to tune them out. Footsteps came close to him, walking up to his bed. Suddenly blonde waves of hair entered his line of vision.

"Hiya, handsome," She looked into his face, and William squinted back at her. "How are you feeling?"

A gurgle of discomfort issued unnaturally from the back of his throat.

"That good, huh?" The woman fell out of his line of vision. There were more sounds and then she was back. "Bit of this will do the trick. You'll go back to sleep real easy. You'll feel better soon, won't ya? In the meantime, I'll take mighty good care of you." There was a prick in his arm, and soon William fell back into a hard, drugged sleep.

There were a few hazy moments of waking up when a similar routine of excruciating pain, drugs, and more sleep continued. He wasn't sure how many times it happened or if he'd spoken or maybe even had sat up, but he was certain above all else that he'd been asked to do things that his body was in no way interested in doing. His vision and understanding of what exactly was happening was fuzzy around the edges. Somewhere in the recesses of his mind, he understood that this had a lot to do with the morphine they were giving him, but it still made his world seem surreal.

During one of those waking moments, no one noticed or cared that he was awake, and no one came to his side. The burning in his head did not go away even if he lay still with his eyes closed. He waited, trying to move his fingers so that someone would notice him, but no one did. William raised one hand, then the other, then let both flop back down.

With great effort, he opened his eyes, licked his lips, and raised his head. He only made it a few inches off the pillow, but that was enough to take a look around him. His vision was still funny. Greens swam into white and reds. Rotating his eyes in their sockets hurt his head all the more. No one was passing by, so he put his head back down before trying again.

"William Sawyer," a female voice sounded closer to him than he'd thought possible since he hadn't seen any females coming or going only a moment before. "Good to see you up."

William opened his mouth and worked his jaw, "Morphine." The word came out sounding as though it had been dragged from the depths below from a place that wasn't supposed to form words. He could hardly recognize the voice as his own.

"Not quite yet. This time the doctor wants to have a word. You just hang in there, and I'll be back soon." The female voice disappeared along with the sound of her footsteps.

William's eyesight wandered around the ceiling of the peak of the large tent that was used as a field hospital. He was moving his eyes to see if certain directions hurt his head more than others, but they all felt like pure misery. His vision was on the edge of focusing, and his entire body was quickly beginning to come alive to him. The haze he had been sinking in and out of since he'd been here was uncomfortably missing.

"Good evening," a male voice came from the same place the nurse's voice had been. Once again, William hadn't noticed his approach.

William grunted.

"Let's take a look at that eye," The doctor moved over him and peered into his face. As he said it, William noticed that what he'd assumed were both his eyes looking up was only one eye. He slowly lifted his right hand all the way to his face and felt the bandage that looped over his other eye and seemed to wrap around most of his head as well.

"How do you feel?" The doctor was still peering into William's left eye.

It seemed to William that it took him forever to slowly open his mouth and let air fill his lungs.

"Not good," William's voice sounded a little less foreign but still groggy.

The doctor nodded at his response then began to remove the bandage that hugged the other eye and his head. "I'll take a quick peek at this one while you're awake." As the bandage fell away from his eye, William closed both tightly. There was an immediate shot of pain that hammered straight into his forehead. "You seem pretty lucid today, that's a good sign. Now, try to open both of your eyes for me. It won't be for long and then I'll have the nurse redress you, and you can keep your eyes closed."

William winced as he did what he was asked.

"Do you know where you are?" the doctor asked as he peered at William.

William was concentrating so hard on keeping both eyes open that he found it hard to even think.

"I'm in a field hospital," he finally said.

"Very good. And can you remember what happened that put you in this field hospital?" The doctor shifted over William's head as he removed the rest of the bandages from his head and peered at it.

William thought back. The sound of gunshots came to his mind, but there was no recognition of what exactly had happened to put him here.

"No," he admitted.

"Do you know what you were doing and what country you were in last?"

Again William tried to think back, but his thoughts were slow. He kept trying to pull up image after image, but they all appeared blank in his mind. "I can't remember."

"What is the last thing you remember?"

"I remember... I remember eating my daily rations in the back of a truck. I think I was somewhere in France." William had a fleeting vision of himself with cold food on his lap. He could hear the voices of other men and feel the bump of the truck, but that was all.

"Can you remember how you got to France?" The doctor's voice was calm, but William could feel that he didn't have the right answers.

He pressed his mind to think, even as his head seared. As much as he tried to push into his mind, he found nothing; a blank nothingness that refused to tell him what had happened.

"No," he finally said. The doctor nodded. William tried again. "Well, maybe. I think I dropped into the ocean, then climbed onto the shore where people were already dying—I think—"

"Ok, that's very good. We'll talk more later. For now, the nurse will redress your head and give you pain medication. You've done well." He smiled in a vague way and then was gone.

Chapter Ten

Grace hummed softly to herself as she walked down a row of wounded and sick men. She'd been moved to the general hospital, which sat behind the front line hospital. It was a different atmosphere. Fewer men died once they came to the general hospital. Their initial care had been given, and with each man who came in, a chart and information came with him. There were answers at her fingertips, names on the papers, and detailed procedural happenings written out by other nurses.

There were fewer surprises here. Grace found herself helping young men who now had to come to terms to a life without legs or an arm. She dressed and redressed wounds and gave the prescribed medicines and treatments. She learned the names of each man. Many sat up talking to their fellow soldiers or talking to her when she was near them.

There was no joy here like she assumed would come in the evacuation hospital. Some men came through quickly, well enough to be moved to evacuation and then straight home. Others stayed. Some for a long time.

Hitler was dead. He'd committed suicide like the coward he was. The war against Germany was coming to an end fast, and everyone knew it. A weighty air of expectancy had fallen among every conscious soldier, nurse, and doctor in their camp. The buzz of a radio could be heard at all times.

Grace grabbed a stack of fresh linens and set them aside. She was starving, and things were quiet enough for her to run out and get something to eat.

"Beulah," Grace found that her voice was practically at a whisper and frowned at herself. "Will you be ok here if I go for some food?"

"Of course," Beulah smiled. She looked at Grace in the careful way that all the nurses had since Matthew died. Grace wondered about the other nurses. She was far from being the only one with a loved family member killed. Alice Reavley's fiancé had died shortly after Matthew. Many family members, sweethearts, fiancés and others were killed or injured for life. It was inevitable. Men were dying in their hospital beds every single day.

Grace smiled briefly at Beulah. "I'll do the linens when I get back." She stepped out of the tent and took a deep breath. The air had a kick to it today. A fresh edge that filled her lungs and swam up her nose. It was only three months until the anniversary of Matthew's death. Soon it would be a whole year, then two years, until...until she was an old woman thinking about her brother, who would always remain young in her mind. And she would always remember the day when Matthew had been removed from this world.

She walked slowly, taking in the day. She watched men walk by with purpose. She heard a group of females talking loudly on the other side of a tent. Grace let her hands lift out to her sides and then fall at her hips. She was stiff and sore from her shift.

She would be happy for it to end, for a chance to lie down and get some sleep.

There was a human cry that stopped Grace in her tracks. It had come from only a few feet away. She stared at the ground as she listened to hear it again. But it wasn't the same sound but other sounds that swept the area around her. People were gathering, moving, murmurs and gasps filling into the air. Grace lifted her eyes but saw no one, so she moved toward the sound.

Her mind was moving too quickly, and her lungs hurt from expectation. She picked up into a run, looking for someone. She ran around three tents, then saw a group of nurses. There was a radio next to them, and one girl was crying silently on the ground. Two others were embracing one another, silent and solemn as they listened.

"What is it?" Grace asked.

"Listen," another female voice said from behind Grace. Grace turned and stared at the face behind her waiting for more.

There was a crackle on the radio. Winston Churchill's voice could be heard decidedly over the airwaves…"This is your victory…We have never seen a greater day than this…" There was a cheer, and "God bless you all."

"What does that mean?" Grace turned to the woman who had appeared beside her. "Is he saying—is it over?"

"It's over." Tears were flowing down both plump cheeks of the woman who Grace had never met. A loud roar was quickly spreading through the camp. Grace turned toward the filled tents, the soldiers pouring out in a frenzy of celebration, some walking in disbelief, others jumping and shouting. An American flag was raised by a clump of soldiers. Grace felt herself half-ready to fall over and half-ready to jump with the rest of them.

Grace felt her knees give way, and the girl next to her grabbed Grace by the shoulders, sitting her gently on the ground as she sat down too. Grace stared at the girl, and the girl buried her face into her hands as her body worked its way into racking sobs.

Grace bent over the ground. It had been an emotional few days, but Grace had forced herself to stay strong until it was final.

Now, the air was sucked out of her lungs. She placed both hands on the dirt in front of her, bracing her body. It was over. The war was over. Grace stumbled up to her feet and walked forward into the growing number of people. The noise was growing so loud that it was becoming hard for Grace to hear any distinctive words at all. A man grabbed her by the shoulders, then pulled her into his arms, swinging her around into a mad dance. She found herself laughing with the man before breaking free and moving again. She was bounced between bodies as she walked. Hoots and cries were loud in her ears.

She moved back into the tent, her eyes searching for Millie.

Turning and spinning, the tears in her eyes blurred her vision. Soldiers were throwing things in the air from where they sat in bed. Others, who were able to get up, stood. Some men leaned on their crutches, dancing just as enthusiastically as those with all their abilities on the other side of the green canvas.

Grace's eyes fell on her friend. Millie was wrapped in a man's arms, kissing him. She pulled back in the throes of laughter.

Millie caught sight of Grace and ran to her, scooping Grace up into her arms just as the soldier had scooped Millie.

"It's over!" she yelled into the loud fray of noise. "It's all over! The war is over in Europe. They have surrendered. We won!"

Seeing Millie touched something in her. Grace felt fresh tears tumble out, and a new, heavy sob knocked the breath out of her. "Oh Millie," she sobbed as she jumped and spun around the floor with her friend.

Millie was soon lifted into another man's arms. Millie had flirted her way through every sick and hurting man, and now they all wanted to swing her around, embrace her, and kiss her. Grace smiled at the sight, then walked through the crowd and din until she was at the far end of the tent, through the flap, and into the empty compartment where they kept supplies. Her stack of linens still sat, untouched, as if nothing had happened. Grace held onto the table in front of her.

"It's over, Matthew," she said to the empty room. "It's over."

Chapter Eleven

When the enormous machine of the western war began to move, men were sent home as fast as they could be moved. Grace volunteered to stay on in Europe, caring for the men who could not yet be moved home. She liked to think that she just wanted to stay to help those who needed it, but she knew the truth. Facing her parents, going back home, and facing a house without Matthew in it would be unbearable.

She would be forced to do it one day, one day soon, but she couldn't manage the idea that the day for facing her home had already come.

The effusive happiness that had filled Grace boiled down as the days went by. Her happiness was replaced by the thought of Matthew, her longing for her brother, and her hurt that he'd not made it through to see Hitler dead and Germany brought to its knees.

Once her field hospital had been packed up and moved out, Grace was moved to another general hospital. As more men were moved out and the tents were taken down, the remaining men were filtered into the better hospitals, the ones that had been hospitals before the war, the ones in real buildings. Grace was moved to an old church that had been turned into a hospital during the war. She found it strange to be inside a stone structure. The beds were lined up neatly in their rows. There was a real kitchen, and the food was better than it had been when they were on the move.

The biggest surprise and the best part of the new hospital was the real bed she was given to sleep in by the nuns who lived in the building next to the church. She was hesitant even to sleep in it, afraid to waste the luxury to sleep.

Grace was free to go for walks through the countryside and the nearby town. After such a long time of sharing space with another person every moment of every day, she was finally able to breathe, to get away on her own and spend some time in the peace of her own mind.

~

William was able to open his one eye without the same solid wall of pain. He'd been told that he'd hit his head before falling straight over the bridge during the battle of Remagen. He had floated a few hundred yards down the Rhine before hitting a bank where another American soldier pulled him out of the water. His head was badly injured, he had a broken leg, three cracked ribs, and a dislocated shoulder when he made it to the field hospital later that day.

He would have been ready to leave for a hospital in the States after only two weeks, but as he was being moved, there had been an accident in the truck in which he was riding. His already fragile and broken body had been thrown against the side of the truck, which meant a longer period of recovery in Europe before he was safe to transport.

William had already been suffering severe memory loss before the truck accident. If his head were compromised again, there was a possibility of permanent brain damage. The doctor put William in bed to stay. He wasn't even allowed to stand up out of bed until a week after VE Day because falling posed too great a risk.

He spent most of his time staring up at the ceiling with his one eye. His mind went naturally and easily back to his childhood. He began to have visions of his father before his death. He thought of his mother and grandmother trying to make a life after his father had committed suicide. The old childhood anger, hurt, disappointment, and shame came crawling back into his waking hours of idleness.

After he'd been able to sit up for some time, he'd begun to listen to those around him. Speaking and even listening still gave him a headache, but the sound of someone else in his head made him feel better.

His head was still in horrible pain every day, and though he was unable to do it himself, sometimes a nurse would make time to read to him. They found the black Bible among his things. William couldn't remember packing the Bible, bringing it, or reading it. That wasn't such a surprise since he couldn't remember the battles he'd been a part of, the friends he'd had who might have been killed, or even how he'd come by the various injuries that he'd accrued along the way.

One man, who'd been in the bed next to his for almost a month, told William that he was lucky for this. The man woke up every night in spasms of panic and fear. He dreamed of his friends being shot down next to him every night, over and over again. He said that if he could, he would choose not to remember anything that had happened since the war began.

William knew that he must have similar memories. He must have been through the same things. But they never showed in his dreams. Only his father made an appearance in his dreams now, and he'd been dead for thirteen years.

Every day William felt that he was looking through a large hole in his mind. Although he might have agreed with the man if he knew what it was that he was forgetting, he hated the absence. He wanted to remember his life. He wanted to remember what had happened to him in last few years. The absence of so many events and years scared him. He felt that with his head injury, part of his life had also been removed.

When William was finally allowed to stand, his muscles were weak. He could barely walk around the hospital on his own.

Then, gradually, his body began to rebuild strength. His head was still wrapped, his leg still required crutches, his ribs were sore when he laughed or coughed, but his shoulder had healed quickly once it had been put properly back in the socket.

William took his new ritual walk – or hobble – around the hospital and was back to his hospital bed. He plopped back down and exhaled at the effort every little thing took. He'd never realized how much he'd taken for granted – his health, mobility, and ability to do things without facing an incredible migraine.

He picked up his Bible and opened the pages. He couldn't read them himself. Reading or focusing on anything too much lit his head on fire. He could stand it for no more than a minute or two before closing his eye with an appalling headache that lasted the rest of the day. So, William just pressed his fingers to the pages and felt the weight of the book in his hands.

Though he couldn't remember why a Bible had come into his possession, he felt it must mean something, have some significance.

When he looked up from the black cover, his eye fell on the slight figure of a woman he'd never seen before. She was bending over a man who had been critically injured only days before the war ended. William often woke up to the sounds of the man crying. He had been severely burned down one whole side of his body. From one side of his bed, the man looked almost normal. On the other side, however, the skin had melted and turned into something unrecognizable as human.

The woman was putting medication on the disfigured side of the man's body. William couldn't take his eyes off her. She looked like an angel. The soft outline of her face, the way she tended the man without a hint of disgust. She looked him full in the face just as if he looked like any normal man. She smiled at something the man said then turned back to her work.

William watched her until his head was in such acute pain that his vision was turning into a smeared picture.

He was sweating from the pain, his body shivering. But seeing her had been worth it.

Grace walked around her new hospital trying to make herself familiar with her new surroundings. She spent two full days in the old stone church and two luxurious nights sleeping on one of the real beds the nuns had given up.

"What shall I do?" Grace asked her new chief nurse after she'd finished feeding a patient who'd lost all use of his extremities.

Ruth, the new chief nurse, was a stout woman who appeared to be constantly in a bad mood, but Grace had learned within a couple of days that this was only a ruse. She was really one of the kindest and most gentle women that Grace had ever met.

"There's a soldier in bed twenty, William. He's leaving us tomorrow, heading home, but one of us usually reads to him when we can. Just until we do medicine rounds though, because I'll be needing your help." Ruth went back to writing on a soldier's chart in front of her, and Grace nodded serenely. There'd never been time for reading to soldiers on the front lines and hardly even in her last general hospital. There had always been too many things going on to do more than share a few words while she'd worked on the patient.

Grace looked over the beds as she began walking slowly to number twenty.

A man was lying back with his head thickly bandaged. He had one eye free of bandages and that eye was closed. She had no intention of waking the man up to read to him and was about to leave, when the man opened his eye.

Grace smiled and took a step toward him. "The chief nurse told me to read to you for twenty minutes. Would you like that?"

The man's open eye was such a lovely dark blue that it startled her into staring at it. He had a slightly pronounced cleft chin and a strong jaw. He was a little thin from lying in the hospital, but Grace thought he normally must cut a fine figure of a man. He was so handsome that Grace immediately looked down to her hands and away from his gaze.

"Would you read me the Psalms?" The man's voice was low, and Grace thought he was speaking to her in a gentle way, a way she wasn't used to hearing.

"Oh, yes." Grace looked at him, surprised by the request, though she probably shouldn't have been. She pulled a chair over to the bed. "My mother had me memorize many of the Psalms when I was a girl. They're beautiful, poetry really. I understand why you like them. When I first came overseas I used to say them to myself to help me fall asleep." The blue eye was trained on her face, and Grace blushed hot.

"Would you say them for me? Just as you did when you used to go to sleep?"

Grace shifted uncomfortably. The request felt personal, and she could hardly look at him when she thought he might be thinking of her sleeping form.

Grace hadn't used them to help her sleep since Matthew had died. She hadn't said any verses at all, hadn't read anything from her Bible. She had tried to pray at first, but her anger overtook her, and she found she couldn't go on. So she just stopped trying.

"Wouldn't you rather a novel or—something?" Grace looked around her but only saw the plain, black, leather-bound Bible. It looked just like the one she'd been given as a girl, and a kick of apprehension pounded in her belly. She did not want to touch it. She did not want to open those pages even more than she didn't want to recite the verses aloud.

"I don't have any novels," the soldier said. He was looking at her still, and Grace took a soft breath. "But I won't make you recite anything if you don't want to."

"No, I don't mind," she lied. Grace smiled, took a breath, and leaned back into her chair. She closed her eyes but still felt the gaze of the handsome soldier on her.

"This is from Psalm 19..." Grace took a breath and let the words flow out as if on a slow, unbroken river. "The heavens declare the glory of God; the skies proclaim the work of his hands. Day after day they pour forth speech; night after night they reveal knowledge. They have no speech, they use no words; no sound is heard from them..." She continued on all the way through Psalm 19, Psalm 23, Psalm 91, Psalm 51, and Psalm 16. When she'd finished, she opened her eyes to find the soldier's eye closed as well and a single tear dripping down the side of his face.

Grace felt a sudden pang for the man and was thankful for the verses her mother had given her, thankful that she hadn't read to him from a novel after all. This man, no matter what she felt, needed consolation of a kind she could not give. The kind that only a greater being could give. Only God could give.

She reached out a hand and gently touched the warm surface of his skin. He didn't flinch at the feeling or the unexpectedness of it, but on the contrary, seemed to anticipate it. She smiled at the look on his face and the emotion he showed. She'd seen many men show lots of emotion since she'd begun in the field. She'd never known men felt so much, could cry from overwhelming feeling and not just pain. Her father, though loving and caring, was stoic. She'd never seen him cry or even come close to it.

"Would you say them again?" The brilliant blue eye opened and looked right into hers.

She wasn't sure what time it was or if she was due to gather and dispense medications with Ruth soon. But the look on the soldier's face was in such earnest that she couldn't make herself say no. Instead, she squeezed his hand and gave him a small nod. She sat back, letting go of his hand. She watched as he relaxed into his bed, once again closing his eyes.

"The heavens declare the glory of God..."

Chapter Twelve

Grace and Ruth were the last nurses to leave the hospital for good. They'd stayed an additional seven months after the war in Europe had ended to tend to those who couldn't travel. Then they helped pack up the hospital and helped restore the little church to its normal state of being.

"I bet your parents will be happy to have you home," Ruth said. She and Grace were travelling with the last three soldiers to a military plane that had been used throughout the war as an air hospital. There would be others flying with them as well.

"And I'm sure your family will be happy to have you home too," Grace said as she gave Ruth's arm a pat. Given all the time they'd spent together, and the fact that they were the last to leave, they'd become closer than Grace had been to anyone else throughout the war. Grace had lost tabs on Millie but assumed she was home by now, happily flirting with all the men in Boston.

Ruth was old enough to be Grace's mother. She had been made a widow in the World War I, before she'd had any children. She'd never remarried, but she had her sister and her sister's family waiting at home for her.

"You are always welcome in Granite Falls," Grace said to Ruth, though she knew the older woman was not likely to take her up on the offer.

Ruth nodded a bit and said, "And you will always be welcome in Charlottesville."

Grace nodded thoughtfully. The closer she got to home, the more nervous she became. She was nervous to see her parents, to see her brother's old friends, those who were still alive, that was.

Everything would make her think of Matthew. Everything already made her think of Matthew. She couldn't even handle her own grief, how would she ever be able to handle her parents' grief?

Her parents would be tucked snuggly in firm arm of the church. They would find comfort in God. She was sure of it.

It scared Grace to go back home with her new doubts, with her anger. How could God let something like this happen? How could there be a war like this when a supreme being was in charge? Wasn't God supposed to be without fault? Wasn't He supposed to be all good and just? If that were so, then how could he let this happen to a man like Matthew? Matthew had been such a strong believer, just in the beginning of his life. He had complete faith until the day he died. So how had God let this happen to him of all people?

"We'll be there soon," Ruth said as they passed a sign for the airfield.

"Good," Grace looked at the open fields around her. There was a small house to her left that looked abandoned. She watched as they drove past a wooden fence that was falling apart. The land looked ravaged. It had been ravaged. The ground was blood-soaked. One day she would come back here, Grace decided. And she would see the land the way it was meant to be seen.

Chapter Thirteen

"William Sawyer," a loud male voice rang out at him from across the street. William turned toward the voice. William saw a large man approaching fast upon him. Without warning, the man gave him a large, tight hug, then pushed him back and looked him over.

William had gained his strength back. His head had been healed enough to remove the bandages for good. Only a long scar ran over his scalp where hair no longer grew to show the damage that had been done to him. His hair was cropped short to his scalp for now, but soon he would let it grow out so that it would cover the scar.

"How are you? I heard you'd come back." The man was ruddy-faced and smiling widely at William.

"I'm good," William tried to find some of the same enthusiasm the man was displaying but found only a deep-rooted panic instead. This had happened to him a few times already since he'd come home.

There were holes all through his memory. William had no idea who the man in front of him was, but he was sure that he'd been someone that William had known well before the war. "And how are you?"

"Jack died, but you'll have heard that," The man's face became serious. William nodded solemnly.

He found it impossible to ask the pertinent questions or to explain what had happened to his memory. He'd tried to do that the first time it had happened, and the woman who was talking to him had looked so hurt that William had decided that he would just pretend from then on.

"I'm sorry to hear it," William said.

"You're looking great. I heard you were injured, but you look right as rain." The man gave William a looking over. William smiled and nodded, looking down at himself.

"I'm working ok," He tried to sound positive again.

"Good to hear it," The man gave William another hug. "I'll be seeing you real soon." The man gave William a quick look then barreled off toward an old, prewar truck.

William watched him go. He'd lied, of course. He wasn't ok. He almost wished it were his body that was letting him down instead of his mind. Not knowing who or what he should know was almost more than he could stand. He'd told his mother and grandmother, of course, but nobody else.

When William got home, he had decided that he wouldn't mention the run-in with the man to his mother. His mother, though she understood, seemed to find these lapses so unsettling that she would go off to clean the kitchen for an hour before speaking to William again. He assumed her reaction had something to do with his father, that William's problems were mental like his father's had been. Since his father had been mentally unstable enough to kill himself, his mother probably put them together somehow, though William couldn't see a strong connection himself.

His mother was out of the house when William got home, and he was secretly glad.

"Hey Gran," he said to his grandmother as he walked past the living room. His grandmother was listening to a program on the radio and rocking herself gently in a wooden rocking chair William's father had made her.

"Hello, Villiam," Though she tried her best to hide her German accent, her "w" still came out sounding a bit like a "v."

"Do you need anything?" William queried from the doorway.

"No, I am quite well." She continued her rocking and looked at her grandson. Their family hadn't talked much about the war. Though his grandmother insisted her allegiance was with America, and she pushed herself forward as one of the great patriots of their neighborhood, William knew better. She had family still in Germany. At least she had before the war. Though she didn't approve of Hitler or what was being done in Germany, there were still the familial bonds that pulled at the seams of their conversations. She couldn't know if her family was alive or dead. Had her nieces and nephews been killed? What had happened to her sister or the people she'd grown up with? The truth was that William himself could have killed any young, male, German relative without ever knowing it.

William walked on to the kitchen. He'd spent the day working at Johnson's Pharmacy. He had worked there since he was a child, and they'd been able to give him part-time work now that he was home. He enjoyed sliding back into his work there. It was one thing that hadn't left his mind.

He went to the kitchen and made himself a sandwich for lunch. He would need to change and get a move on if he was to make it to the Tuesday night prayer group he'd begun to attend. It was another aspect of his life that his mother didn't understand or particularly like. She knew little about it and was naturally wary of his new interest in the Bible, prayer, and God. He'd tried to talk to her about it, but she'd changed the subject, and he knew not to press her. She was adjusting, just like he was.

She'd sent a son away to war as one person, and he'd come back as another. He'd lost chunks of his memory, he had new burgeoning beliefs, and he was becoming a person she didn't recognize anymore.

~

"We're really glad that you made it tonight," Patty said, standing in the church rec room. She was putting on her small summer hat as her husband was talking to another member of the prayer group. Patty and John were in their late sixties. John had a confidence in his faith that William was jealous of. He spoke with certainty, and he was never afraid to pray aloud or talk about his relationship with God. Patty had brought a huge plate of cookies this week, and now she was sending William home with the leftovers — a task which he was happy to oblige her.

"How did you start?" William asked impetuously.

"Start what?" Patty looked up at William with surprise and curiosity.

William looked over the wall behind her then shifted his eyes back, "Start believing."

Patty's eyes held on to William's, and she seemed to consider him for a long while.

"Well, I was lucky. My parents were very strong Christians. They both had a wonderful relationship with the Lord, and that's what they passed down to us. They raised me and my three brothers with God at the front of every decision." She considered William again, "But John wasn't so lucky."

William turned and looked for her husband who was laughing with another man, both walking slowly toward them.

"Both of his parents died when he was young. He lived in New York back then, a son of immigrants." Patty looked at her husband, "He was a brave child. He was sent out on one of those orphan trains, came here, and was taken in by a farming family to help on the farm. They were nice enough people, but he still felt abandoned—felt the loss of his own real family. The family that took him in treated him well, gave him food and shelter, put him in school through the winter, which is more than he would have gotten by himself on the streets of New York. But he never felt like one of their children. He never felt like he had a family."

William felt a surge of surprise. He would never have thought the confident, Godly man to have come from a less than happy place.

"When he was older, he went to a church dinner because it was free. He was pretty poor then and needed a good meal. That's where he heard about Jesus. It took some time, but as he came to know God and the scriptures, he realized that the father and family he'd been missing so much had been with him the whole time, he'd just never known it."

John and the other man were at the door now, and they both stopped their own conversation and turned to William and Patty.

"I was just telling William your story," Patty said to her husband. "He was asking how I came to believe."

John turned his eyes to William. He was a large man, as tall as William, but broader, with a thick neck and large facial features. The older man's high forehead scrunched as he looked William over.

"You've been through a lot, I think," John said as if he was gazing into William's life.

"Nothing unusual, these days," William said.

John nodded. "Why don't you come to our house for dinner tomorrow night? We're having a small dinner for two of our friends. They've spent their lives as missionaries around the world. You might find it interesting—plus Patty is making her world-famous pot roast, not the sort of thing you want to miss."

"World-famous?" Patty gave her husband a little look, but William could tell she enjoyed the compliment. "We are having a lemon meringue pie for dessert," she said in William's direction.

William looked from Patty to John, making sure they were really inviting him. Then he smiled.

"What time should I be there?"

Chapter Fourteen

Grace sat motionless on the small antique chair. Her eyes were fixed on her mother.

"She's coming here? Now?" Grace asked. She began to pick at her cuticles, and her mother immediately gave Grace a reproving look.

Since Ethel Finley had taken in the news of her son's death, she'd dropped back from her normal outgoing activities in the town and taken to her own household. Matthew Finley Sr. had found solace outside of the house, in his work. He'd begun working more, spending early mornings and late nights at the office. Since Grace had come home, both parents had been making an effort for her, but she felt their strain and understood it all too well. Without her work, she had no outlet, nothing to pour herself into, nothing to take away the constant thoughts of Matthew.

After Grace had only been home a week, Ethel informed her that she'd invited Trudy Padgett over. Trudy was the mother of Jimmy, the young man Grace had seen die under her hands about a month before her brother's own death.

"I won't know what to say to her," Grace said, looking to her hands. She didn't want to talk to yet another grieving mother. She didn't want to tell another sad story.

"It will mean a lot to her. When you wrote about Jimmy—later—well, she's wanted to meet you ever since. It will only be for a quick tea and talk and then you can be off." Ethel's eyes were plaintive, and Grace understood that it wasn't her mother's idea. She could feel that Trudy was the one who had pushed for the meeting, and that her mother had only had the strength to give her daughter a week before putting the two face-to-face.

It occurred to Grace that the two mothers had both been members of the Blue Star Mothers of America Club when both of their boys were alive, but now they'd both become members of the Gold Star Mothers of America Club. They both had sons who had died in the war. It was a membership that Grace was certain neither mother wanted.

"I'm just going to powder my nose." Grace stood up abruptly.

"Grace, dear, she'll be here any second," Ethel said as she looked up at Grace with a sigh of exasperation. Her mother, who had once been so patient, even overly nurturing, was now too exhausted for such things. Grace could feel her trying, but her mother just wasn't the same.

Nor would any of them ever be the same again, Grace thought.

"I will only be a few seconds. Tell Mrs. Padgett that I will be right back," Grace looked at her mother and smiled. "Ok?"

"Very well, dear." Ethel gave a soft smile, and Grace walked out of the room.

Standing in front of the mirror in the tiny, first floor, powder room, she splashed a bit of cold water over her face, trying to gain courage for the conversation ahead. She hoped her mother was making the tea strong.

When she walked back into the room, Trudy Padgett was standing in an embrace with Ethel Finley. Grace watched the two women who now shared a sad and devastating history. Trudy opened her eyes and saw Grace. She stepped back from Ethel as if she'd felt an electric shock.

"Mrs. Padgett, I'm—so sorry for your loss." Grace moved forward and took the woman's cold hand in her own. "I know how inadequate those words are, I've heard them too many times myself, but I don't know what else to say anymore." Grace looked the older woman in the eyes and immediately saw the same sorrow that Grace felt every day.

"Won't you sit down?" Ethel held out her hand and waited for Mrs. Padgett to take off her light summer coat and her gloves and then handed them to Grace to put away. Grace sat down last. She looked over the table to see that everything was there, hoping that there might be something in the kitchen that was needed for her to find.

"Grace, you can sit here," Her mother indicated the only available chair.

"Of course," Grace sat and poured out tea for her mother and Mrs. Padgett. There was a heavy silence, an invisible intruder listening in and sitting at the table with them. "So, Mrs. Padgett, what did you want to know?" Grace kept her voice soft, though fear ran through her.

"I…" Mrs. Padgett started as she looked into her teacup, "…I don't really even know. I guess—I want to know everything." Her eyes filled, and one tear fell directly into her freshly poured tea.

"Of course," Grace said. Her sympathy and pain went out to Mrs. Padgett, though Grace didn't really know what to say or how to say it.

Grace picked up a large mound of sugar and eased it into her dark tea. She spun the mixture around a few times before looking back up at Mrs. Padgett.

"Your son came in one night, I don't really know when, but another nurse came over and told me there was a boy from Granite Falls," Grace said in one breath. "So naturally I went over, and there was Jimmy. He—he'd been badly hurt." Grace looked into the eyes of the other woman, trying to determine how much she wanted to know. Everything. Mrs. Padgett's eyes told Grace that she wanted to know everything.

"He'd lost both legs beneath the knee." She paused to let this information sink in. Grace didn't know how much information the Army had sent home. "But, he was very upbeat about it. We talked about home. I told him that he would likely have a parade in his honor. He would have to…we talked about you, Mrs. Padgett, and how you and my mother met for meetings, how you went out delivering food to families who'd lost a son."

Grace licked her lips and took a breath as Mrs. Padgett pushed a napkin to her eyes. There would be no stemming of the tides from those eyes today, Grace thought as she watched the fruitless task. "I believe that he was very proud of you.

"I told him that he would be going home soon, that he would go to a general hospital, then an evacuation hospital, then a hospital in the States, then home. When I came back…the next morning to check on him before I left my shift, there was something wrong. He wasn't conscious anymore. I talked to him anyway—about you and home—then I prayed for him. I prayed that if it was the Lord's will to take him that Jimmy would go in peace."

Grace watched the woman's face, which now shown red around the edges of her nose, eyes, and high up into her hairline. "I think the Lord answered my prayer, Mrs. Padgett. I think Jimmy went in peace. I think I was there to help give him comfort in the end."

Grace exhaled, and her shoulders fell away from her ears. She looked to her own mother who was also in tears. Grace sat between the two crying women, trying to keep herself from crying as well, though the tears had lifted into her throat, threatening to break free at any moment.

It was a long time before anyone left the table. Questions were asked that had already been answered, but Grace took the time to answer them again. When Mrs. Padgett left the house, Grace went straight to her room, laid face down on her bed with all of her clothes on, and fell into a deep, dreamless sleep.

When she woke up the next morning, something within her had changed. She didn't know why or how, but she knew that she had to leave Granite Falls. She needed space to recover herself. At the same time, she was worried for her parents. She didn't want to leave them broken and alone.

She spent the day walking around Granite Falls, looking up at the trees the way she'd seen her brother do so many times before.

After three hours, Grace knew what she wanted to do. She put in a long distance phone call and then headed back home for dinner with her parents.

"Hello, dear," Ethel said as Grace walked into the kitchen.

"Can I help you with anything?" Grace asked. She looked around for plates to take out, dishes of food, or silverware that hadn't been laid.

"You don't have to," Ethel said, turning back to the stovetop.

"I want to," Grace picked up the plates and took them out to the table.

When everyone was seated, there was a silence around the table. Grace was sure her mother was still thinking about the day before, about the conversation with Mrs. Padgett. Her father was often quiet, and Grace didn't feel ready to bring up the decision that she'd come to only two hours before.

After making their way through the main dish with nothing at all said, Grace took the plates back to the kitchen and sliced a small cake her mother had made. She put each slice on a small plate.

"I talked to a friend from my last hospital today," Grace said abruptly as she sat back down to the table.

"Did you?" her father asked, his wild eyebrows raised.

"Yes," Grace looked between the two. "She, well, she's a bit older than me and… she offered me a job."

"A job?" Grace's mother was suddenly a part of the conversation as well.

"Yes, she works at a hospital in Charlottesville, Virginia. Only about a six-hour drive or so. I would live with her, and I would visit you on every break. Every holiday. I would be making enough to get a car—after a few months. A cheap one, but…"

Grace put down her dessert fork looking between the two people who had raised her, whom she loved so much, and who had always shown their love for her.

"I—don't have to go of course, if you need me here." She suddenly felt wracked with guilt for abandoning her parents when they needed her the most.

"Do you think this is what God is leading you to do?" her father asked, and Grace looked up into his eyes.

"I don't know. I'm finding it hard to… I think I just need some time. With Matthew and… I think it might be good for me." The words made her feel like an utter traitor, not only was she leaving them, but she was abandoning the very God they had taught her to trust her entire life.

"We want what's best for you, Grace." Her mother's voice was soft, and Grace felt the cool, papery skin of her mother's fingers cover the hot skin of her cheek.

Grace lifted her eyes slowly to her mother and then took her mother's hand and kissed it.

"Your mother is right, we want what's best for you always. If this is it, then we support you, Grace."

Grace looked to her father and felt the thick ball of emotions creeping slowly up her throat.

"We just want you to do it with God." He looked at her. "Don't try to do this alone. It is the hardest thing to lose someone you love. Far too difficult to go through on your own. God is with you, don't shut him out."

Her mother's words sang out as Ethel stroked her daughter's cheek, "Go with God's grace, my child. Go with God's grace."

Chapter Fifteen

The next day, William felt oddly nervous about his scheduled dinner. He looked through his black, leather-bound Bible, pulling out small pieces of scripture. It was still difficult for him to stare at or read anything for too long, but the pain in his head had diminished greatly, and he was able to focus for much longer than he'd been when he'd first come home.

John 14:6, *Jesus answered, "I am the way and the truth and the life. No one comes to the Father except through me."*

William stared at the passage. How did a person go *through* anyone? Besides reading more, he had recently begun going to Sunday morning service. Still, there were so many things he didn't understand.

He closed the book and went downstairs to make his grandmother tea.

When he got to Patty and John's house, he knocked apprehensively on the front door. It was hardly ten seconds before it swung open and a face he'd never seen before looked out at him.

"I'm sorry, I think I have—"

"You're in the right place," The man pushed the screen door open. "The women are in the kitchen, and John is getting a record that I apparently 'have' to listen to," The man smiled and held the door for William to walk through it. The man looked the same age as John and Patty. "You must be William?" The man asked.

"Yes, sir." William looked around the living room. It wasn't fancy, but it was cozy and immediately felt like a home. A deep sofa sat against one wall, a coffee table with a few hors-d'œuvre set out on it claimed the middle of the room.

"I'm Stu, by the way. Terrible of me not to introduce myself right away." The man made his way over to a large side chair where he sat down. William followed his lead and sat on the couch across from him.

"Army, was it?" Stu asked as he leaned forward and picked a little tart-looking thing off the coffee table. William once again followed his lead and took a tart for himself. He took a bite, and his mouth filled with the taste of mushrooms and onions.

"Yes, sir." William said after swallowing down his first bit of mushroom tart.

"Please don't call me 'sir.' I would think you'd have had your fill of that in the Army." Stu said with a lopsided grin.

"I suppose I did…." He was about to say sir again but didn't. He also didn't feel like he could call a man so far his senior by his first name, so he just cut himself short and didn't call him anything at all.

William picked up another tart, which could easily have been a one-bite sensation for him, but he took a polite two bites instead.

"John said you were a missionary?" William realized that he had no qualms calling John by his first name and John was about the same age as Stu. Probably because everyone else in their prayer group called John by his first name too.

Stu nodded. "Yes, I met my wife in Paraguay. Lived there for seven years, helped to build three churches, and spread the word. Africa and Asia as well, but we moved back to the states when the war was starting. Too old to fight but not too old to help on the home front."

William nodded, wondering what it would be like to live in Africa, Asia, or South America.

"Was in the Army myself during the first war," Stu nodded. William could see Stu's eyes glaze over the way they did when someone was back in the fields, back in the middle of explosions and gunshots. "I lost these two, but I was lucky to come out with my life." He lifted his right hand, and William noticed that Stu was missing his ring and pinkie fingers.

"I had a head injury," William said, gesturing briefly to the thick, ropey scar that still showed through his hair. "That was the only thing permanent—"

Stu nodded, looking at William's head as William turned his head in Stu's direction.

"I suppose I was lucky to come out with my life as well. They tell me I was close to being drowned when they pulled me out of the river. Been through a good number of other battles too, I'm told. Got this," He pulled up his sleeve to show another gash that would one day fade to a scar, "but I can't remember how."

"You lost some memory from that?" He gestured with his chin toward William's head.

"Almost all of it, from the moment I dropped into France until I woke up after," William gestured again to his head. "Other parts are missing too, people, places, events from before the war. It's been—really frustrating."

Stu nodded, "Sounds like it. Will any of it come back?"

"They said it probably would in its own time, but they also said it might not. So far, nothing has really resurfaced, so I'm not convinced that it will."

"Found it," John came plodding into the room carrying a record in his hand. "William, glad to see you! I hope you tried those little things," he said, wagging a finger at the little tarts that were on the table.

"Had two of them. Too good to pass up," William smiled at the way John was always talking up his wife's food.

"Glad to hear it. Have two more." John came all the way into the room and scooped up a tart as he moved to the record player.

"Now, I'm willing to bet five dollars that William here has heard this song." John said, pointing his finger at William, which made the younger man laugh.

"Of course he has, but I'm sixty-two, and I've been listening to the same songs for the last forty years."

John laughed loudly at this, "At least he's willing to admit it, eh, William?"

William couldn't help but laugh in response, not because the comment was so funny but because of the enthusiasm John gave it. He put the record on his player and set the needle. The first few strains came across, and now William did laugh because of the content and not just because of the funny little dance moves John was making across the floor.

The Andrews Sister's began to play, "Rum and Coca Cola." John danced to the rhythm surprisingly well. Just as he began to sing along with the music, Patty and another woman came bursting into the room.

"Oh John, not this song again." Patty was holding a spatula, and the woman behind her was laughing behind her hand.

John ignored the particular sound in Patty's voice and took her, apron, spatula, and all into his arms and began dancing her around the living room. Patty could not help herself and quickly let herself be danced around.

"You're a really ducky shincracker, John," Stu said loudly over the music as the large man danced on.

William sat back into the sofa and watched the spectacle. The woman William hadn't met gestured to Stu, who refused to be moved. William took the opportunity to look at the woman who was presumably Stu's wife. She was olive-skinned with thick black hair pulled up on her head in Rita Hayworth's latest style.

The woman surprised William. He'd assumed that Stu had meant that he'd met his wife in Paraguay, not that she was from Paraguay. He'd assumed Stu would have married a nice, white, missionary girl from Kansas, but this woman was totally different. She was more stylish than most of the women in town, with bright red lipstick that went well with her skin. She was beautiful and at least ten to fifteen years younger than Stu.

When the song ended, Patty pulled away as if she'd been completely coerced into dancing in the first place, though she'd obviously been enjoying herself.

"Dinner is ready, gentlemen," Patty said to the room at large. "That is, if you are able to pull yourself away from the Andrews Sisters for a few minutes."

John promptly turned the record player off and gestured to both Stu and William to lead the way into the dining room.

There were family pictures along the walls, though William hadn't heard anything about the couple having children.

Dinner was perhaps better described as a feast than a meal. Just when William suspected the food was about to stop coming, there would be another dish brought around. A basket of soft, warm rolls was placed in front of him. Suddenly, as he looked down at his plate and his thick slab of pot roast, William was reminded of a song. Someone had been singing about pot roast and corned beef and spam. He remembered the song. He remembered being in a tent and the deep baritone voice that sang it. William stared down at the meat as the small blast of memory came back to him. He couldn't remember the face of the man who'd sung the song, but he knew he had liked him.

William pulled at the threads of memory until he was sure they had all disappeared. That was it. That was the first memory that had blossomed for him out of the emptiness. William hoped there would be more. There must be more. In the moment that it had come, William hadn't been thinking about much at all—the food that was being passed, the way it smelled, and the way it would taste. Perhaps that would be the way. Perhaps it would take years, the rest of his life, for all the memories to come back to him.

"—everything ok? Can I get you something?" Patty's voice broke into his thoughts and William looked up. She'd been talking to him, and he hadn't even noticed.

"Everything looks great," He smiled at his hostess, who looked at his plate then walked to the sideboard where she set the dish that she'd just divvied out.

Patty and the other woman took their seats, and everyone automatically bowed their heads.

"Lord," John's voice was reverent but simple, "we thank you for this food that you've provided for us, which Patty and Sol so lovingly made. We thank you for the presence of our old friends and our new friend. Help guide William's heart toward you. Protect him, Lord. Keep him strong, open his mind to your glories, and show him the path you've made for him. In God's name, we pray." Then from everyone around the table, "Amen."

Chapter Sixteen

William walked home from John and Patty's house with competing thoughts vying for attention in his mind. The fact that he'd remembered something was incredible. It was only one thing and only a little bit, but it was hope for more. If he could remember one thing, then why couldn't he remember everything?

The prayer John had said also buzzed around in his brain. He'd never had anyone point him out in such a way. He'd never known anyone who would willingly, voluntarily intercede with God for him. To ask God to guide William personally felt like an honor he was not worthy of.

There was a warmth in the air tonight that was far from oppressive. A soft breeze drifted in and lifted the air off of William when it became too hot. It seemed like the perfect confluence of heat and cool. William saw his own street but decided that he would continue to walk on. He passed his road and walked down a tree-lined lane.

The houses only one block over from his own house were worth four times as much. It was easy to see why. They were beautiful. The lane was beautiful. Heavy blossoms dropped to the ground, covering the grass in pink and white. A smooth, flowery scent floated around him, and he felt safe and protected here in this lane with the gentle wind that now brought cool air with a sweet, intoxicating smell on its breath.

"What am I to do now?" William said aloud. Thief River Falls no longer felt like the right place for him. He was back at the pharmacy only part-time. The job had paid enough before the war, but now he had additional skills, and he could look elsewhere. Plus, the part-time pay wouldn't be sufficient for long.

There was also the fact that he was being constantly approached and reminded of his mental insufficiencies. Everywhere he went, he was afraid of people. Afraid that when someone looked his way, he was supposed to recognize them. Then when he did recognize someone, he was afraid that he didn't remember their story correctly... or his own, for that matter.

He couldn't live in fear of people for the rest of his life. It wouldn't be right. He wanted to walk freely into the future without fear of the past.

But how did a person do that? William put his hand out as a blossom floated to the ground. He gently intercepted it with his hand. He looked into his palm steadily. The blossom was proof of something. Proof of God, maybe? How could such a thing come into existence without God? The intricacy of the bloom was too unique, too amazing when looked at from this perspective.

How many things had he been overlooking for his whole life? Too many. That was most certainly the answer.

William exhaled, then inhaled fully as he made his way down the lane. He'd remembered a song tonight. He'd remembered a voice. He'd remembered a tent. That was something.

William folded his hand around the blossom and tucked it gently into his pocket. If he was going to move freely into the future, then he ought to begin remembering to look at the amazing, the overlooked, and the fantastically unique things he'd been taking for granted his whole life. He'd been given a new chance at life just by coming out of the war alive. It would be a shame to waste it now.

Tomorrow, he decided. He would ask John what he thought. He would ask John about moving and about a new job. He would ask John to pray for him.

Chapter Seventeen

"Ruth!" Grace exclaimed as she jumped out of the bus and into Ruth's open arms.

"Don't you look nice in a dress!" Ruth said, beaming at Grace as if Ruth were a proud parent. "I was so surprised when you called, but I'm so glad you did! My old house is lonely now that I got used to the tight quarters of field living. I can't tell you how nice it will be to have a warm body in the house. Someone to talk to over dinner!"

Grace smiled a heartfelt, genuine smile. She felt light and free. Perhaps it was being away from war, away from the battlefields, and away from her parents. She'd never been out on her own. Of course, she had Ruth, so she wasn't really alone even now. It just felt nice for her to make her own decisions and follow through on them.

"I think you'll like your room. My sister helped me to charm it up a bit and make it a little more age-appropriate."

"You shouldn't have gone to so much trouble," Grace reprimanded.

"It was no trouble at all. I just hope you like it."

Grace looped her free arm with Ruth's, and said, "I am positive I will."

There was no mistaking that she missed Matthew terribly. She was aware that she needed to spend time mourning his loss, but she still felt strangled by her anger, hurt, and loss every time she thought of him. She was unable to breathe properly, unable to even move sometimes. Maybe, just maybe, she would get a few days, weeks, or even months of distraction. Maybe a new job and a new town she'd never even seen before would help.

"What do you think of Charlottesville?" Ruth asked as she motioned her hand around the center of town.

"I love it. It's gorgeous." Grace looked over the buildings and the greenery that surrounded her. It was beautiful.

"I'll take you to the hospital tomorrow where you can see where you'll be working. Everyone is so nice. There's a nurse-training program, which you'll be helping with a lot. I have a feeling you'll be an excellent teacher. After all your experience, it will be good for you to share some of your knowledge."

Grace took in a deep breath of fresh air.

"Of course, you'll be helping with the patients too," Ruth walked on, leading the way. "I think you're going to like it here."

Grace nodded and said , "I think so too."

The first two weeks were a flurry of activity. Grace had been right, she was distracted. She poured herself into her new job at the hospital and helped make dinner every other night with Ruth. She even began to make some new friends of the other nurses at the hospital.

Grace was finishing a long shift. She'd had a non-stop day of helping patients, and now she was exhausted, almost too tired to walk all the way back to Ruth's house. Despite her fatigue, she was happy. She'd talked to a good number of nurses, doctors, and patients. She felt useful, like she was doing something good in the world, *and* she was making her own money. Knowing she had the ability to pay her own way in the world was marvelous. She'd always thought that being an Army nurse would be the end of her working; that she would come home to a husband, have a few lovely, chubby babies, and call it a day, but Grace truly enjoyed her work and didn't want it to stop.

There was a constant smell of green in Charlottesville that Grace couldn't get enough of. As soon as her nose hit the outside air, her exhaustion floated off her body. She felt the energy of the nature around her and quickly felt alive again.

A soft wind ruffled her hair and skirts. As she moved across a grassy walkway, Grace looked up and stopped.

An overwhelming sense of Matthew instantly flooded her, and she was unable to move the slightest bit forward.

"Matthew." Her lips moved, but no sound came out. In front of her, crossing her path, was boy of maybe eleven or twelve. His face, his walk, even the expression on his face was just like Matthew's had been at that age. She was almost sure that if she went to see him up close that she would see the pale freckles on his nose, the clear blue eyes, and the scar that went across his eyebrow. But Grace didn't move. Logically, she knew it wasn't him, but for the moment, she didn't want to be contradicted out of her thoughts.

Grace watched the boy walk. She wanted to hear him talk, to hear someone say his name. Quickly, without really thinking it over, Grace changed course and followed the boy. Her heart thumped, and her mind lay somewhere between the impossible and the supernatural. Was it possible that she was going crazy and that no one else saw this boy who marched in front of her?

Grace looked at the people he walked past, and they noticed him well enough. No one walked into him, and everyone else seemed to realize he was there. When she got to the end of the next block, she stopped following him. She watched him cross the road and walk away down the street.

The excitement that had overcome her now left. It wasn't Matthew. Of course, it wasn't Matthew. It was a preposterous thought. Grace closed her eyes.

As she opened them again, her gaze roamed across the street. A small stone church stood proudly on the corner.

Her eyes looked from the small stone cross on its peak, back down to the two wooden front doors. A pang struck inside of her. Church had always been the place where she'd felt the safest and where she'd spent years feeling loved and cared for. She longed for the safety of it now but hated the thought of taking something she still wasn't sure about. Something she'd been avoiding and scrutinizing since Matthew had died.

Grace swallowed the emotions that had welled up in her from the vision of the boy who looked so much like Matthew. She moved her head to both sides as she looked for traffic then quickly crossed the street. She stared at the building for a long time. There were lights on inside, and she thought there might be a night service. She thought that maybe if she just slid into the back, no one would notice. Her skirt swished around her legs, and her heels clicked on the stone steps.

Grace reached out a hand and wrapped her fingers around the large brass handle and slowly pulled.

The door was open. Grace walked in slowly. There was no one in plain view, so Grace stood in the center aisle looking up toward the pulpit. Her eyes floated over the decorative wooden cross and the flowers that were probably left over from Sunday's service. The church was relatively plain on the inside, and that made Grace feel even more at home.

She walked in two more steps and moved herself into one of the pews. Her eyes looked to the wooden cross. She let herself sit back into the pew, resting all her weight into it.

"God," she whispered, "I don't know what I believe or how all this is going to work out." She stared for a long time listening to her own breath, feeling the solid strength of the pew beneath her. "It's just—I miss Matthew." A tear rolled down her cheek, and she closed her eyes again.

The church was quiet…or rather, nearly so. As she sat with her eyes closed, Grace heard a soft noise coming from the far side of the church. Choir practice was the first thing that came to her mind, but she realized it wasn't voices singing that she was hearing, but rather voices speaking.

Grace stood up out of the pew. There was a tug pulling inside of her. She felt herself being drawn forward, if by curiosity or by God, she wasn't totally sure.

She moved all the way down the aisle, then to the left of the pulpit. Her old church used to have stairs that led deeper into the church, into the choir room. Grace walked all the way to the side until she saw a similar set of stairs.

Putting a hand out onto the banister, she walked quietly down the steps. At the far back, directly behind the choir benches, was another door. This one was more modern than the rest of the building appeared to be. There was a small window at the top of the door, and Grace saw a hallway beyond it.

One of these rooms was probably the choir room, and the others were probably Sunday school classrooms or maybe a fellowship hall. Grace turned the knob on the door and let herself into the carpeted hallway. At least here, her shoes wouldn't give her away. She walked slowly back along the wall, glancing into the little windows on the doors now and again. On her right, she saw a bulletin board, and she stopped, staring up at it.

There was a flyer for a potluck dinner in two weeks' time, a notice about Sunday school classes for children and grownups, a special prayer meeting, and down in the corner was a notice for a young adult Bible study. "Ages eighteen to thirty," the flyer said. "Thursday nights at six."

Grace looked down at her small wristwatch. It was six forty-five. So that was where she'd heard the voices come from. Out of curiosity, Grace turned into the next, much shorter, hall. She walked past another darkened room, then caught sight of the light shining from the small window in the last room.

Grace walked stealthily up to the lit window. She suddenly felt like a Peeping Tom or some sort of ne'er-do-well. She peaked around the edges of the window, but the people in the small room were all facing away from her. She breathed out a tight breath and moved forward, letting herself move right up to the window now that there was little threat of being seen. There were perhaps thirteen people seated in a circle of plastic chairs. They were all around her age or a bit older.

She watched as a few of them laughed, and yet another seemed to be debating something hotly. Grace's eyes suddenly flicked up. There was one face not looking away. One face that was looking directly at her.

She felt her cheeks burn hot as she realized the man who had been looking at her was one of the most handsome men she'd ever seen. He stood without anyone else noticing and began walking toward the door where she stood.

Her stomach dropped rapidly. She felt like an idiot. How could she possibly explain her presence here? She'd just walked into a church that wasn't even hers. She'd heard voices and then just followed them for no apparent reason.

Grace frantically turned away from the door and sprinted in her dress and heels to the bend in the hallway and then back up the corridor. She heard the door close and then footsteps behind her. She opened the door to the nave and slipped inside. Back up the stairs she went and down the center aisle. Grace gave one last look back and then hurried out into the night.

~

Had he felt her presence or had he just turned around at the right time and noticed a figure in the doorway? He'd seen her before she'd seen him. He had been staring like an idiot, of course, when she did notice his gaze. Why had he stared at her like that?

He knew why. Any man would be blind if he didn't stare. She was so lovely, it was startling. Arresting. She was the most beautiful woman he'd ever seen. Just by looking at her, he felt that she was already familiar to him. Though the same mustn't have been true for her because she'd immediately turned on her heels and run away.

William stood outside of the main church doors looking down both sides of the street. She was gone.

Something inside of him was whistling for his attention. He could barely catch his breath.

Was it possible? What he was feeling? He'd only just seen her. He hadn't spoken to her, hadn't interacted with her, yet there was this feeling. The bursting, pressing, burning feeling was that the girl he'd just seen, the girl who'd run away from him, the girl in the peach colored dress…was the girl he was going to marry.

The feeling was there, all right, but it was nonsense. It had to be. He'd never met the woman before.

He didn't know who she was, and now, without a trace, she was gone.

Chapter Eighteen

She had been standing on the other side of the door. Illuminated in the small window that had been built into the wood. There was the sound of laughter on his left and the voices of a debate on his right, but William felt removed from them. He was outside of everything going on in the world. There was a separation that included only him and the girl. Her eyes flicked to his, and then she turned. He saw it perfectly, as if she were in front of him right now.

"Sawyer," his partner's voice cracked into his consciousness. William turned toward it. "Visiting the girl again?"

William had told Jones about the girl he'd seen. He'd been able to think of nothing else. Every day he thought he saw her. He saw her walking down the street, in a car, sitting at a table getting a hamburger and shake. Every time he followed her, he would touch her on the shoulder, before realizing he'd been wrong.

None of these women had been the girl he'd seen in the church building. Some had similar hair or wore their dress the same way. Others had nothing in common with her at all.

William hadn't discussed his memory issues with the police captain or with Jones. His memory loss from the war wouldn't impede his work on the police force, so he didn't see that it mattered. He'd told them about his general movements during the war as they'd been relayed to him. He was far from the only man who didn't like talking about the war. Many men wanted to put it behind them.

Jones had been on the other end of the war, fighting the Japanese. He'd mentioned a few bits of his history, but the story had been cut short when he'd told William about losing his older brother. The Japanese had taken his brother prisoner, but on the way to a POW camp, the group was bombed. The American bombers didn't know there were any American prisoners with the group of enemy soldiers.

"We've got a call—domestic disturbance down on Azalea Drive," Jones gave William a thump on his upper arm that got him moving. He was back in the real world, his vision of the girl tucked into the back of his mind.

The two men had been walking the University of Virginia campus and now jogged to their Ford. The new car was a beauty. A shiny black body with a long nose. William threw Jones the keys and ran around to the passenger side.

Jones did not turn on the siren. It was late, and most of the town was sound asleep. There was barely any traffic, and they would be at the house within a minute or two either way. When the two men pulled up to the pale peach cottage, everything was quiet.

"What did the call say?" William asked, looking at his partner.

"They said there was yelling. Someone thought they heard the man hitting his wife," Jones squinted at the house. "Apparently this isn't the first call on this house."

Both men strained their ears but still heard nothing. A creeping feeling began stirring in William's brain. William put a hand out to stop Jones, and he turned to his partner.

"Let me go first." William wasn't sure what it was that was coming over him. He felt a sudden need to protect the man on his right. Henry Jones, who he'd only known for a week now, had shown every sign of being able to take care of himself just fine, but William felt a burst of panic for the other man.

Jones stared at William for a few seconds and then nodded. "Sure," he said.

William walked in front of Jones and ascended the rickety staircase that seemed to be rotting away beneath him.

He listened again then knocked loudly on the door. There was no sound from inside.

William motioned that he was going to take a look around the house. Jones nodded his agreement as he began walking in the opposite direction. He was planning to walk around the other side of the house, but William felt the same panic come over him.

"Jones," William motioned for him to come back and follow him. Jones paused for a moment, looking at William quizzically again but still decided to follow him. William knew that his actions would seem strange to Jones, but right now he didn't care. He just wanted to make sure Jones was safe, no matter how strange it made him look.

As he stood looking out at the trees in the neighboring yard, a flash came back to William. It was a dark night, he was behind trees, and there was a man next to him, motioning for him to wait. William was listening for something then, looking for Germans. He couldn't remember anything else, just the chill of the air on his face, the feel of his helmet on his head, and a map that had been in the other man's hand. William felt sick.

The memory clenched at his heart and at his stomach. He wanted to push it away, and at the same time, he wanted to drink it in. William swallowed back the memory—he had to focus on where he was now. He had to be in the real moment.

He turned on his flashlight and looked into the first darkened window but saw only the backside of a curtain. He and Jones continued through the dewy grass to the next window and found the same thing. He felt the strain of the current circumstance along with the past twisting his muscles at the base of his neck. His body was bracing. He needed a moment to relax, to release the tension that had inserted itself inside his body. But that moment wouldn't come out here in the middle of the night.

The back of the house showed a small concrete platform that led to a door. The backyard was barren. Where there might have been grass, there was only dirt, and the sight of it made William inexplicably sad. Now that the cloud cover had moved on, the moonlight was streaming down.

William stepped up onto the platform and shined his flashlight into the back window. A kitchen sink and counter came into view. He moved his flashlight again. The beam of light hit something on the ground. William moved his beam around the floor. It took a moment for his eyes to adjust.

"Is that a woman?" Jones' voice was just behind him.

William moved the beam and then nodded, saying, "I think so."

He handed the light to Jones who held it while William used his sleeved elbow to break the glass. There was a soft shatter, and then William reached through the hole and unlocked the door from the inside. His fingers instinctively reached for the inside wall and found a light switch. The kitchen illuminated in a yellowish wash that spread over a dull green and white kitchen.

A woman lay on the floor, her head on the ground and her arm draped over her head. William reached for the woman, "We'll need to get her to the hospital." Before he even said it, Jones was calling in for an ambulance.

As William gently turned the woman over, he could see that she'd been beaten badly. Her face was turning blue in various places as blood dripped from her nose. He thought that some part of her face might be broken. He lifted her wrist and felt for her pulse. It was there. Slow, but she was alive.

There was a noise next to him and William turned to see a dog in the doorway. The dog was tied up and looked close to starving. William wouldn't be surprised if the dog had been beaten as well by the soft whines and yelps it gave in William's direction.

"I'll go do a check of the house and see if the husband is still here somewhere," Jones' voice made William looked up.

"—No, I'll go. Stay here with her." William stood. His strong protective instinct was still controlling his interactions with Jones.

William made his way out of the kitchen, moving with caution. The house was dark, and each room he entered required that he find the lights and flip them on. He kept his pistol in his hand, unsure of the behavior to expect from a man who beat his wife unconscious and starved and beat his dog.

The darkness enveloped him as he moved upstairs. Again, there was a flash of memory that came back to him in the darkness. William stopped in the middle of the staircase. His chest was moving heavily. He felt like a large man was sitting on his chest, keeping him from getting a full breath.

William stood still as he pushed his hand over his heart.

He closed his eyes and tried to bring himself back to the staircase. He wasn't in a German forest. He was in a house in Charlottesville, VA, where he might run into an angry man at any moment. His eyes opened again, and he peered up into the darkness. He could see the outlines of the wall and a banister. He hadn't been able to find a light switch for the main hall, so a general outline was all he was guaranteed.

He moved up the stairs and then stepped on the landing. There on the wall was a light switch. The entire entryway filled up with light, and William exhaled a pocket of air he'd been holding tightly in his lungs.

There was no one else upstairs. The husband must have left.

William grabbed a wedding photo of the couple from their hallway wall. He and Jones could run by the local bars after they'd gotten the woman to the hospital. The whole thing reeked of a boozed-up battering. The ambulance was pulling up just as William came downstairs. They were only a few blocks from the hospital, so it would be a quick ride.

"We'll want to question her when she's awake," Jones was handing the driver and his assistant a card with the headquarters phone number on it.

The two men left from the back door with the woman securely strapped onto a stretcher.

William raised the photo of the couple. Both were in their formal wear and had bright, sunny faces beaming at the camera. The woman was barely recognizable without the discoloration and broken face. The man looked like he could have been a movie star. HIs smile was straight and perfectly charming.

Jones turned toward the open door, looking about himself for anything important that might have been left behind.

"What about him?" William looked down at the dog, and Jones followed his line of vision.

"What about him?" Jones asked.

"We can't just leave him here, he's half-starved to death and probably gets kicked around as much as the missus." William bent down and held out his hand to the dog. The dog didn't move for a long time, but then slowly, cautiously, he moved forward. "That's it, I won't hurt you," William's voice dropped to a soft coo.

"What would we do with him?" Jones asked.

William looked at the dog's large, dark eyes and felt a twinge for him.

"I'll take him home. When the woman wakes up, we can give him to her or find out what she'd like to do with him. I can't leave him here with this guy." He gestured with the picture. "Plus if we take this guy in, then who's gonna feed him?"

Jones shrugged, and William untied the end of the rope that was anchoring the dog to the floor.

The two men and the dog left the house and loaded into the Ford. The dog wasn't interested in getting into the car so William let him sniff around and take his time. Then William carefully picked him up and put him, whimpering, in the car.

"I'll grab a burger or something at the bar," William said as he thought aloud.

"We just ate. You can't be hungry again already?" Jones turned to William.

William looked down at the brown, furry body next to him and said, "For the dog, Jones. For the dog."

Chapter Nineteen

Grace pushed a long strand of hair back into place. Her hair had grown substantially since she'd come home from Europe. She secured the strand with a pin and then looked back at the chart she was reading for a patient in room 32.

"Hey, doll," Grace heard the voice behind her and turned around. Nurse Cindy Rogers was standing behind her with a large grin on her face. "Whatcha up to after your shift?"

"Oh," Grace blinked. "I'm… nothing." She wasn't feeling much in a social sort of mood, but she couldn't think of an excuse fast enough.

"Me and a bunch of the gang are going out for sodas. We've decided that you are coming along." The other nurse smiled as if she'd played some sort of trick on Grace and then put both hands on either side of her hips. "What do you say?"

"Well, it's been a long day," Grace started pushing through appropriate excuses in her mind. She didn't want to be rude, but she also wasn't prepared to go out with a group of girls who would invariably talk about the frivolous and ridiculous.

"That's exactly why you should be coming out with us. Meet you in lobby after you get off," Cindy winked and then turned and walked back to her station. Grace stared after her. The other nurses were always going out together. They spent breaks together, gossiped, talked about heaven only knew what, and generally showed an interest in each other that went well beyond anything Grace could imagine participating in at the moment.

She'd been happy with Ruth's company. Though Ruth was much older than Grace, she was quiet and had just the sort of old familiar patterns that Grace could get on board with. Ruth was always saying that Grace should be going out with girls her own age, but Grace felt removed from everything frivolous and "fun." It felt wrong for her to fuss and gab when her brother was dead and her parents were heartbroken. She was grieving and heartbroken herself, and there was always the knowledge that Matthew wasn't able to shirk off the rest of life and just be a young person like Grace was supposed to be doing.

Matthew *had* no life.

Grace turned back to the chart in her hands. She could think of no way to get out of sodas, so she would go. She could tell Ruth, who would be happy, and perhaps it would get the girls to stop asking her so often. She wasn't even sure why they did ask. It wasn't like she was fun to be around.

As Cindy had promised, there was a small group of girls waiting in the lobby when Grace came down from her shift. Grace had taken her time thinking that Cindy might forget and leave without her if she didn't show up right away. But as soon as she stepped into the lobby, Cindy turned to her with a smile. Grace smiled back. She couldn't help it.

The group consisted of Cindy Rogers, Katherine Smiley, Beatrice McLaughlin, who everyone called Beau, and Ginger Stanek. Grace made a fifth.

As soon as the group left the hospital there was a buzz of talking and laughter. The girls all seemed so happy, maybe just happy to be done with work or maybe happy to be with one another. The light talk and tinkle of laughter was actually nice, and Grace found that she liked being inside the group more than she'd expected. She sighed as she listened to everyone around her.

"So sugar," Beau said to Grace. "What's your story? Where are you from?"

Beau had flaming, bright orange hair with freckles to match. Her wide hazel eyes fell on Grace, and she smiled with interest.

Grace was surprised to feel her cheeks grow hot from the attention. She'd been under the radar for so long that it felt strange to have a group of people all listening to what she had to say.

"Granite Falls. It's a small town in North Carolina." Grace looked to the pavement then back up to Beau.

"You have family here?" Katherine asked over her shoulder.

"No, I worked with Ruth Westerly during the war. I'm staying with her now." All the girls knew Ruth.

Katherine nodded, "Ruth is a real good egg. She's the one who trained me when I came here. I'm from Idaho."

Grace looked up, "Oh, I just figured that you were all from here."

Beau laughed, "Only Ginger. I'm from Alabama, but I try my hardest not to sound like it."

Grace looked at each of the girls trying to reassess her initial impressions of each one. "So, what brought you all to Virginia?"

"My aunt lives here, and I wanted something different after the war." Beau's face was somewhere between her normal laughing face and a serious one. "The city where I lived back home was… well, it just wasn't the same."

"I didn't know a soul here, just knew there was a good hospital where I could work." Katherine's voice was precise and matter of fact. "There were no hospitals that I wanted to work in back in Idaho, and my boyfriend—well, he didn't make it through the war so…" Katherine's voice choked up, and Ginger placed a tiny hand on Katherine's back. "I just decided on a place completely new."

Grace nodded. She'd not realized that many or even most of the girls who worked in the hospital all felt the same way she did. They'd all been through the same things, all lost people in the war, and they had all experienced their cities and towns being shaken up and not put to rights. Grace felt a twinge of regret for her prior attitude toward the girls. She'd just assumed that because they acted peppy that they were actually happy girls.

"So," Ginger said in a voice that was committed to rallying the group. "Did any of you see the guy in room 17?" Ginger smiled and looked around her.

"Osweiler?" Beau crowed back at Ginger. "He has teeth as big as my hand," Beau held up her hand as a visual aid.

"I think he's cute," Katherine said to Ginger, more in defense of her taste than in actual feeling toward the guy.

Ginger blushed crimson, "He does have sturdy teeth, but have you heard him laugh? It's to die for."

Grace smiled at the girl. Ginger seemed like the youngest of the group. She was tiny, with bones like a bird. Her hair was worn in large loops on either side of her head, which made her look a little disproportionate.

"Ginger is bonkers for the boys," Beau gave the tiny girl a poke in the ribs, and Ginger yipped.

"I am not. I only think he's handsome, is all," Ginger pulled herself up to her full height, which couldn't have been more than a clean five feet, and tossed her head.

"She's ready to settle into some strong man's loving arms and produce a snuggly little baby or two," Beau moved in front of the group, turned to face them and began walking backward.

"And what's wrong with that, I'd like to know?" Ginger turned to Grace, and Grace smiled.

"There is nothing whatsoever wrong with that," Grace cooed at Ginger, who blushed at her words.

"What about you?" Ginger asked with a hesitation that Grace found charming.

Beau's voice pounced over Ginger's, "Yes, what about you? Are you keen on having a husband and baby with big chompers?"

"No," Grace said too swiftly. "Not that I mind big teeth," Grace looked to Ginger. "It's just…" She felt herself trailing off without a thread to pick back up.

"Just what?" Cindy pulled into the conversation. She'd been distracted by something behind them and had just run to catch up with the group.

"I guess I just don't have it in me right now," Grace didn't like the sound of her own answer, but she also didn't have anything else to add. She couldn't imagine telling all of these women about Matthew. She wasn't sure they'd understand anyway. It wasn't like Matthew was a fiancé or husband. He'd been her brother. But, even the thought of loving someone as much as she loved Matthew, even the mere possibility of having that person taken away—it was too much.

Cindy looked to Katherine, who shrugged over Grace's answer, and then turned to Beau.

"There's a lamppost behind you," Katherine said with a straight face to Beau, who spun around to find that Katherine had been lying. The girls broke out into giggles, and Katherine walked with a champion's gait forward to the soda shop. She held the door open until Cindy moved up and grabbed it.

All five girls plunked down into a four-person booth, which didn't much matter as Ginger was tiny enough to count as half a person, and all the girls were small anyway.

"I'm going to have a root beer float," Cindy announced loudly. A few heads in the diner turned at the new arrivals and then turned back to their own food.

"Oh Cindy," Katherine turned to her. "You never have to worry about your figure, do you?"

Cindy lifted her shoulders then winked mysteriously, "Not when there's a root beer float in the picture."

"The moon is so bright," Ginger looked out the window and all of the other girls followed her gaze.

"Do you see what I see?" Cindy whispered as she looked out of the window. Each girl turned to follow Cindy's line of vision. Across the street stood two uniformed police officers talking animatedly to each other. Then suddenly one of them burst into laughter.

"Hey, I recognize them, they're the ones who came to check in on that dame...you know the one in a coma after her husband beat her. That one," Beau pointed her finger, and Katherine quickly bat it down. "The one on the right, the handsome one. He brought her dog to see her and everything. Keeps coming back to question her, but she got the living daylights knocked right out of her. Might not ever wake up."

All the girls at the table looked across the street with greedy eyes. Grace watched them with a smile then turned toward the window and squinted as she tried to see the police officer Cindy was talking about. Grace stopped when she began to recognize his face.

The man across the street was the same man she'd seen in the church. The man with the strong jawline and the eyes that had looked so deeply into hers.

Grace immediately turned away from the window, afraid of being caught out staring at him through yet another window. She rearranged herself as she sat in the booth, looking first to the table in front of her and then to the couple who sat to her left. Grace's eyes and face were moving but her thoughts were on the man on the other side of the street.

When she couldn't stand it any longer, Grace turned and looked back at him. He didn't seem to notice that he was being stared at by five women just on the other side of the street and behind a pane of glass. Grace watched him as he moved. His hands moved in front of him as he talked to his partner. When he talked, his face moved on an angle, and Grace got a better view of him.

Some feeling grabbed at her stomach, and she pulled in a breath. He was so handsome. The coincidence felt almost fated, and the thought scared Grace. The other girls were all talking about him, but Grace hadn't been listening. She began to tune in, trying to pull her attention away from the handsome man across the street.

"I hope I'm on the next time they come in," Katherine said with wide eyes.

"He was mighty friendly with me the last time he came in," Beau tossed her head lightly. Ginger's face fell.

"Don't worry," Cindy spoke straight to Ginger. "I bet he's nice to everyone."

Grace stood abruptly, "I'm going to run to the ladies' room." The group all turned to look up at her.

"Ok," Cindy said surprised. "We'll be here."

Just as quickly, they all turned back to the window. Grace walked through the booths. Her heart was hammering, which made no sense at all to her.

Grace ran the faucet and patted her face with cool water. She looked pale in the mirror as she stared into her own eyes.

"No," She traced her the lines of her face in the mirror, seeing the same nose and jawline that she would have seen on Matthew if he were standing in front of her. "None of that for me—" Her eyes lifted until they matched the eyes in the mirror.

"You've had enough heartbreak for one lifetime."

Chapter Twenty

Grace hadn't gone out again with the group of nurses, but she did find that the one outing had changed her view of them. She realized that they were not so different from her after all.

As she'd been making her rounds, Grace's mind went back to the police officer she'd seen twice. She was taking the vitals of the woman in the coma that the officers came to visit. Grace wrote each stat in the woman's folder, Marjorie Daniels was her name.

Marjorie's face was swollen out of shape and discolored, her hand was in a cast, and Grace thought it was probably for the best that the woman wasn't awake to feel all the pain that surely sat in her body at that moment. Grace checked her chart to make sure she'd had a sponge bath and been turned enough to keep bedsores away.

A garbled sound made Grace turn. Grace watched as the woman's lips moved. She was waking up.

"No, no, just—" Grace clapped a hand over her mouth. She couldn't believe that her first instinct was to wish the woman back into a coma until her shift was over. Grace swallowed back the words and gave herself a stern mental reproach.

She walked to the door and caught sight of a bright orange head.

"Beau, she's waking up, we need a doctor," Grace called to the other nurse. Beau took a moment to understand what Grace was talking about, but once she did, she backed away from the door she was about to go into and jogged away from Grace down the hall.

Grace turned back into the room and moved to the woman.

"Everything's ok," she said, brushing the woman's hair away from her face gently. "You are safe in the university hospital." She understood that it had been the woman's husband who'd caused this damage. Grace couldn't help but wonder what would have happened to the woman if the police hadn't come to her house and found her this way. Would she have died? That seemed the only real possibility.

Grace's heart was fluttering for more than just the woman. Grace knew that Beau would be sure that the two police officers who'd brought the woman in would be notified. She just hoped that she'd be long gone by the time they came in.

"Harrogld," The woman's lips kept moving, and Grace tried to put the sounds together into some semblance of a word.

"Don't trouble yourself, you can say what you need to later," Grace told her as she began checking the woman's stats again. The woman's eyelids lifted and closed like a butterfly's wings trying to break free of a spider web.

The woman's lips kept repeating the same sounds, and Grace tried to hear the sounds as a word. She bent over the woman as her eyes opened fully and wide. The sight of the woman's panicked eyes startled Grace.

"Harr- gold?" Grace repeated, seeing that the woman would not relax until Grace understood her. "Harold? The name, Harold?" Grace asked and saw the original panic leaving the woman's bloodshot eyes.

Marjorie began to speak again, and Grace exhaled, wishing the woman would just relax.

"Is Harold your husband?" Grace asked. She could see by Marjorie's expression that Harold was indeed her husband.

Grace nodded, "Don't worry. We won't let him hurt you here."

Marjorie's eyes changed, and her mouth began to move. "Wahn harrgold ear," Marjorie obviously felt the pain of moving her mouth. Grace began to move back. She was going to check on the doctor or at least get her more pain medication. But as soon as Grace moved, the woman let out a guttural cry, and Grace moved back to her. Marjorie kept repeating her sounds until Grace put a hand over Marjorie's hand.

"You want Harold here, with you?" Grace asked. The woman relaxed, and Grace's heart sank. This woman actually wanted the man who had done this to her to come and sit with her. To stay by her side. Grace nodded, trying not to let her dismay show.

"Marjorie?" The doctor came in with a swift flurry of his white coat. "I heard you were up," the doctor talked to her as if he'd spoken to her a million times before. He was an older man with eyebrows that made all the younger nurses giggle. Beau walked in behind the doctor and looked over at the woman.

"You'll stay here?" Grace asked Beau, who nodded happily. Grace left the room with a deep breath. Beau could do all interface for the woman. That would suit her just fine.

Grace walked to the main nurses' station and stopped halfway there. In front of her was the man. He was out of uniform, and he was staring directly at Grace. He must have been on his way here.

She tried to look away from his gaze and could feel her face growing hot all the way to her ears. She couldn't decide on a spot to look at so she kept shifting her focus from thing to thing as she walked closer to the nurses' station.

"It's you," he said when she was close enough to hear him. She looked up at his words. So he recognized her.

"I'm sorry?" She tried to look nonchalantly at him but felt like she must be failing miserably.

"I saw you in the church about two weeks ago," he said as he tilted his head and looked at her.

"You must be mistaken, I don't go to church." She tightened her jaw and tried to keep moving.

"No, I'm not mistaken." He smiled at her as if he understood exactly what she was doing. The gaze was unsettling, like her whole self was on display for this man she'd never met. He didn't bother to explain further about the church, because he knew that she knew. She wanted to know how he'd gotten here so fast, but she also didn't want to let him know that she knew why he was here and who he was here to see. Besides, the doctor would want some alone time with his patient before admitting anyone else into her room.

"Is there anything I can help you with?" Grace looked at the man.

"I'm William Sawyer." He held out a hand, and Grace looked at it skeptically.

"Oh," She stared at the hand, then not seeing a way out of it, she took it. His hand was warm and gritty in the way a man's hands are when he uses them frequently.

"And you?" He smiled a charming grin at her, and she looked away from him.

"Grace," she said. She waited until he released her hand then let her eyes find his again.

"Well, it's nice to finally meet you, Grace," William's words made Grace catch her breath. *Finally*. What did he mean by that?

Grace didn't ask.

"Marjorie's just this way. She's up, just this minute she woke up," Beau's voice was suddenly sharp in Grace's ear, and Grace felt a wave of relief rush over her. Beau would certainly dominate things from here.

"She was asking for her husband," Grace found the words had slipped out before she could check herself.

William turned to her. "She asked for him?" His brows creased together.

"Harold? She was asking for Harold," Grace blurted.

William nodded thoughtfully then looked at Grace once more, "You'll be here when I get out?" He pointed to the room. Grace didn't know what to say. She would still be here, but saying yes was tantamount to asking him to find her.

"She doesn't get off for two hours," Beau inserted. She gave Grace a little poke in the back. William nodded then walked forward to Marjorie's room.

"I wonder where the dog is," Beau said when he'd vanished inside of the room.

Grace exhaled as she turned back to the nurse's station, and Beau jogged to stay by her side.

"He likes you," Beau leaned on the countertop looking at Grace with appreciative eyes.

"No, he doesn't," Grace said in a matter-of-fact tone. "He is just interested in the woman, Marjorie," Grace looked to the lineup of folders and pulled the first one. She flipped it open, but her eyes barely took in one word.

"Don't be ridiculous. You have me jealous enough to lock you in a closet," Beau said happily.

"What's happened?" Katherine was just coming on shift. She tossed the remains of an apple into the trash bin.

"Grace has an admirer, and you are going to be beside yourself with jealousy," Beau said to Katherine.

"No, you are not," Grace looked up at Katherine. "Because I do not have an admirer."

"The cop. The one that's been coming in for the coma patient," Beau said quickly.

"Ok," Grace pulled two more folders then turned to go back to finishing her rounds. As she was halfway down the hall, she heard an explosive cackle of laughter. Grace rolled her eyes and continued on.

She kept pushing thoughts of William out of her mind through the next hour. Every time she turned around, she expected to see him standing there, then when he wasn't, she chided herself for thinking about him at all.

"She's sleeping," Grace jumped at the sound of his voice even though she'd been expecting it for so long. "I didn't question her or anything. I can do that later when she's had some time awake."

"Oh," Grace said as she gave a short laugh for her own behavior. "Good, she'll need lots of rest."

"Her face and jaw are too bruised for her to say much anyway." He looked at Grace in the same way as he'd done before, like he was seeing all of her. Things she didn't want him or anyone to see. "It's funny, but I feel responsible for her, after finding her and bringing her in."

Grace shifted her weight. She'd just come out of a patient's room, and she thought briefly about just moving to her next room. However, as much as she wanted to get away, she also didn't.

"That seems natural enough," Grace looked down at the folders in her hands. "I feel the same way about a lot of patients."

"I want to take you out," William said without hesitation. It was bolder than she'd expected. She'd not been asked out much. Wounded soldiers in her army field hospital didn't count. They couldn't stop asking her and any other nurse out. Even Ruth had a proposal of marriage during the war, though no one could be sure how serious the young guy really was.

"I'm afraid I'm rather busy, so that won't be possible." Grace wanted to sound confident in her own decision, but she couldn't seem to stop herself from shifting and looking away from William. William nodded his head as his eyes pierced straight through her.

"Ok," he continued to nod. "I will accept that for now, but I will ask again." He held her gaze for beat, and then he turned and walked away.

Grace walked straight back to the only empty room on the floor. She closed the door behind her and leaned against it. Her eyes closed as her head slid back until it tapped solid wood.

Chapter Twenty-One

Grace. It was the perfect name for her. He couldn't have come up with a better one himself. He'd spent two weeks searching the streets for her. Tapping the shoulders of random women. Now, without any effort, he'd found her.

She was more beautiful up close, more beautiful than anyone he'd ever seen. He'd barely been able to speak when he'd looked up to see her in the hallway. Just the memory of it took his breath away all over again.

William picked up his pace. He'd been going to the hospital on the pretense of visiting Marjorie, but everyone had to know why he was really going. She wasn't there all the time, but he was beginning to learn her schedule, and he was certain that tonight she would be there. Her eyes told him something she was unwilling to recognize in herself, and he didn't know why.

"Come on, Boy." William tugged on the dog's new leash. The dog was growing in girth, and William was glad of it.

Boy stopped sniffing the spot that he'd gotten stuck on and ran ahead of William.

When they'd crossed the street, William tied him up outside of the main entrance, then scratched behind his ears. "Be good, I'll be back." The dog gave one bark then stood watching William go into the hospital.

"Hi Cindy," William said to the loudest of the nurses, who'd also made it a point to introduce herself right away.

"Hi-de-ho," Cindy winked and put both fists on her hips. "Come to see me?"

William smiled and looked down the hall.

"She's in with a patient, she'll be out soon," Cindy said, making William blush immediately. He hadn't meant to be so obvious, especially in front of the loud nurse.

"It's ok, we all know," Cindy said with a sly smile. "Not that it takes much to figure it out." She did an impression of William looking around for Grace that made William laugh.

"Speak of the devil," Cindy said. "Or should I say angel?" She whispered under her breath as she walked out from behind the desk and back through the hallway while Grace came up.

When she saw William, she slowed down and then continued on, trying to seem like she hadn't seen him at all.

"Evening," he said. He couldn't keep his eyes off her. She was perfect and didn't seem to have a clue.

"Hello," Grace smiled lightly at him.

"I was hoping—"

"—Actually, I'm just leaving." Grace cut him off as she picked up a pale grey sweater with intricate flowers embroidered around the edges.

"Which is why I'd like to walk you home," William watched her embarrassed expression.

Grace looked at William, he could practically see her thinking. To his surprise, she nodded her head.

"Good, I'll just wait for you outside," William pointed to the door. He turned and had almost left the building when Cindy's voice crashed down the hall.

"Wait!" she yelled, and she ran with a thud to where William stood.

Cindy held something out in her hand, "Here, take them." William extended his hand, and Cindy dropped a few brown cookies into his hand. "They're dog treats," she said.

William quickly smiled at her. "Thank you." He held the treats tightly in his hand and gave them a little shake, then headed outside. Boy was happy to see William and happier still to have the treats that Cindy had so valiantly procured for him. William was giving Boy a good scratch when Grace finally appeared outside.

"There we go," he said to the dog as he stood up. Grace looked apprehensive so William introduced her first to the dog.

"Grace, this is Boy. Boy, this is Grace." He held his hand out to each. "Grace is a topnotch nurse here at the university hospital," he said to the dog then turned to Grace. "And Boy likes to sniff lamp posts and will eat anything he can, even if it's not food." Grace laughed before bending to let Boy smell her hands. Then she pet him.

"Is Boy his name?" Grace stood.

"No, I didn't know his name until Marjorie came around, so I just thought of him as Boy. 'Here, Boy, come on, Boy, get it, Boy.' So, when I found out his real name is Bogart, I sort of couldn't stop calling him Boy."

Grace looked at the dog, "I think Boy suits him."

"Thank you, that eases my mind greatly." William tilted his head down.

"Besides I think he's more of a Cary Grant than a Bogart," Grace smiled, and William laughed. He'd not expected humor from her. It was nice. Very nice.

"Is he going to go back to his owners?" She looked up at William with a look of concern for the dog.

He hesitated, "I don't know. The husband doesn't want him anymore, which is good for Boy, and I don't want to leave him with that guy. Marjorie is...well, Marjorie is...." He tried to straighten his thoughts out about the wife who had almost been killed by her husband but seemed dedicated to him nonetheless.

"Isn't it strange about her?" Grace's words filled in where William's had left off. "She wants to go back to the man who did that to her?"

"I don't understand it either," William agreed. "She won't even say what really happened. She just makes up all sorts of excuses. It's a strange sort of loyalty."

"So there's nothing you can do?" Grace looked up at him as they walked slowly across the street. He was letting her set the pace, and she was leading the way.

"No, she's saying she remembers running into the door and then falling, as if she did that to herself."

Grace shook her head and sighed. "Are you from here, William?"

The sound of his name on her lips gave him gooseflesh. "No, I'm from Minnesota," he said, looking around at the town he was now a part of.

"I'm from North Carolina," she volunteered, and he looked at her in his peripheral vision.

"And how do you like being a nurse?" He wanted to flood her with questions, to know everything about her. At the same time, he also wanted to just stand and walk with her in silence.

She gestured for them to make a right at the next intersection.

"It suits me. It's the only thing I'm trained to do or have any experience doing." Her voice turned softer, and he felt like she was being taken away from him.

"You were a nurse in the war?" His voice naturally softened from her influence.

She turned to him and nodded, "My brother died. So, sometimes when I'm taking care of other patients I feel like…." She drifted off.

"Feel like you're taking care of him?"

She nodded with a half-smile. "But enough about me. I'd like to hear about your work. It must be an exciting job."

"No. No it's not." He laughed, and whether because of the excess emotion she had been feeling only a moment before or because she really found it funny, she let out a loud, unrestrained laugh, disproportionate to the comment. She clapped a hand to her mouth once the sound came out. Her eyes grew wide, but when her hand dropped back to her side, she was still laughing, and William couldn't help but follow her example.

He became certain in that moment that her laughter was the most intoxicating thing he'd ever discovered in his life and would certainly ever stumble upon in the future.

He waited until her laugh subsided before he dared to speak again.

"What I mean is that, not every day is finding half-dead women or deserted dogs. Most days, nothing at all happens. Drunk and disorderly conduct can be pretty funny, but it's not much of a thrill ride."

She nodded, "That's good, though. That's the way it should be."

They chatted all the way back to her house. When they arrived, she gave a general gesture to the powder blue house in front of them and stopped. "This is where I live."

William nodded as he looked over the house. He liked it. It was a safe neighborhood and was a simple but nicely put together home.

"I could always take you for something to eat, perhaps tomorrow night?" He watched her face and demeanor change again and something in her seemed to shut down.

"No, but thank you for walking me home." She lifted the latch on the gate and opened it.

"If not dinner, then maybe I can walk you home again?" He resisted the urge to reach out a hand to the slender arm that now held the gate aloft.

Her eyes moved from the fence to William, "If you'd like."

She moved through the fence and gently closed it securely behind her. He watched her walk up the path to her house, up the wooden steps, and unlock the door. She looked back at him briefly before entering the house and closing the door behind her.

William turned away and walked up the street. He began to whistle as Boy's tail thumped along.

"It's a beautiful day, isn't it Boy?" The dog's ears perked up as he bounced along the sidewalk with the sun on his back.

Chapter Twenty-Two

To Grace's surprise, William took her words literally. He didn't just come to walk her home, he came the very next day to walk her home. Then he came three more times until Grace was expecting to see him waiting for her after her shift. One time he even came in full uniform, which got a good number of looks from passersby.

He'd made her laugh for the first time since she'd heard of Matthew's death. There was something about him that was so alive. It was something like a magical aura that surrounded him making everything and everyone who came into contact with him better. He seemed to be living more fully than other people.

She hadn't forgotten that she'd seen him for the first time in a church and that he'd been in a Bible study. She wanted to ask him about it, to get his opinions on God and faith. She was actually aching to talk to someone about her own experience but still found it dry on her tongue.

She wanted to know why God would turn his back on her in her dearest time of need. Why had she prayed ceaselessly for Matthew's safekeeping only to have him killed? But she was not ready for such a conversation even if she did want to have it. She wasn't sure she would heed anyone's answers anyway. The answers she could come up within her own head were insufficient to quell her outrage.

Once William had walked her home for the sixth time Grace turned to him. "I suppose," she said, looking at William, whose face looked especially good in the changing light. "I think maybe, that it would be ok if... you wanted to get a coffee." She let the words slip out into the air, tangled as they were. She hadn't really planned on saying it. She hadn't planned on even letting him walk her home again.

Grace had been feeling too comfortable with William, and she felt like what she really ought to do was stop seeing him altogether. But it was just that comfort and ease that had formed that had pushed the coffee invitation out into the air around them.

William looked at her without speaking for a long time.

"Did you just ask me out on a date?" He cocked his head, and Grace blushed right to the roots of her hair.

"No," She twirled around to the gate and opened it. William's hand was out and at her elbow before she had time to walk through.

"Yes, we should definitely go get a coffee." His hand was strong and a whiff of his soap floated to her nose. She felt paralyzed by him. She at once wanted to let herself be folded into his strong arms and at the same time to continue pushing her way through her gate and straight into the house. But Grace stayed, unable to move in either direction.

"Ok," she nodded. William seemed to realize that he was still holding her elbow, and he abruptly let go of it with an embarrassed laugh.

Grace suddenly realized that she could function like a normal human being again. She ducked her head and practically ran up the steps to Ruth's house and into the door. She listened to William's footsteps as he walked away up the street. She could hardly think.

By the time Grace was stepping into the little donut and coffee shop that William had suggested, she was rethinking the whole thing. She knew that she should probably just cancel the date. People got sick every day. It wouldn't be so odd for her to catch an illness. But she'd not been able to gain the courage to cancel on William and had only just enough pluck to show up.

She wore her mother's old pearls that Ethel had given to Grace on her sixteenth birthday. Grace found that her fingers naturally floated to the shiny white orbs. Her thumb slid across one and then another as she subconsciously turned the necklace all the way around her neck.

"You came," William's voice was in her ear, and Grace turned into him. He was closer than she'd originally thought, and when she turned, she found herself only inches from his chest. Grace backed up a step, and William reached out to her waist and pulled her back toward him. Grace caught her breath.

She was about to push William away until she realized there was an old woman walking behind her and William had saved Grace from knocking into her. Grace turned her head and watched the woman go by and then looked down on William's hold on her waist.

William moved Grace again and released her from his grasp. Even when he'd let go, she still acutely felt the place he'd been touching. She tried to brush it off. She was a professional nurse. She'd seen many things in her life, and she'd been able to maintain her cool. She could certainly do the same now.

"We're just going to have coffee, Muriel." William spoke to the waitress as they moved to a small table against the wall on the far side of the shop. Grace looked over the waitress. She was pretty. Young.

A pang of jealousy lodged in Grace's stomach, and she felt an acid mixture tumbling around inside her belly.

"Jones and I come here a lot when we have downtime," William explained as they moved into their seats. "We get donuts and coffee to go, and they seem happy to see us," William smiled. Grace wanted to kick herself for the jealous reaction, but she couldn't because she still felt it. Grace turned and looked at Muriel. She and another girl were both looking in their direction but quickly looked away. So the girls here were the same as Grace's fellow nurses. No wonder they were always happy to see the pair of police officers.

Grace turned back to William.

"You're looking lovely," William's voice made Grace look at him. His eyes said more than his words. He was being sincere, and Grace could see well enough that she had nothing to worry about from Muriel or any other girl. She smiled, despite herself.

"Since the war—since my brother died, I'm having a hard time being close with people." Grace surprised herself by telling William the truth. "It's just that I loved my brother so much. So much. I…" A tear fell down her cheek and splashed onto the table. She pushed her fingers across her cheek and wished she hadn't felt the need to explain herself.

William handed her his handkerchief, and Grace took it while resisting the urge to look at the waitresses again. They were probably seeing all this. She turned slightly into the wall so she was facing away from them as much as possible while she dabbed at her eyes.

"I'm sorry. I don't know why I'm telling you this," she said as she handed him the handkerchief.

He shook his head. "Keep it, in case you need it. I don't think you should apologize for your feelings." He didn't seem panicked or scared of her tears and that made Grace feel even more comfortable. She took a steadying breath and returned her gaze to him, holding the white folded fabric between both hands.

William continued, "You were saying that you've been having a hard time being close with people?"

"I guess I'm just afraid. What happened doesn't make sense to me. It makes everything feel so… unreliable."

He nodded, looking at his own hands thoughtfully. "That's true. Life is unreliable."

Grace took another breath and fought off another wave of tears.

"I think I know how you feel in part. When I was overseas, I had a bad head injury. I lost all of my memory of the war and parts from back home too." He dropped his eyes, "It's strange to have been in something that you can't remember. That's how my mind feels—unreliable." For the first time since Grace had seen him, he looked uncomfortable.

"You can't remember anything?" Grace queried.

"It's not something I'm telling people because I remember everything in the present just fine. I've begun getting clips of memories back, but that feels almost worse. I'm not sure when things will come back to me or what they'll be. Sometimes I get these overwhelming feelings that make no sense, and I just know it has to do with something that happened over there. Something that leaked away from my mind." He leaned forward and showed Grace the scar that lay underneath his hair.

"I had no idea." She lifted her hand and felt the line of the scar. "No wonder you don't like talking about the war." She pulled her hand back to the table as he moved back to an upright position. "Don't worry, I won't tell anyone."

"I know you won't." He gave Grace one of his looks that moved right through to the core of her. This time, though, she felt like they were seeing the same thing instead of her feeling like he was at an advantage over her.

"What has come back to you?" Grace was curious but didn't want to pull any information out of William that he didn't want to give. "Only if you feel comfortable saying," she added hastily.

"Nothing remarkable. I get these little scenes, darkness, a sense of waiting. I see one or two things, then days later another thing will appear in the same scene. More than anything, I get this overwhelming sense of feeling, presumably what I was feeling at the time."

"Do the doctors think more will come back to you?" Grace tried to imagine what it would feel like if she couldn't remember anything that had happened during the war. It was impossible to even imagine.

"Yes. Mostly they think it will come back in the next few years, either slowly, or all at once, but there's a possibility that it will just be gone forever. Then I would be living like I had some sort of hole in my head." He ran a hand across his face as if he were physically wiping away the thought.

"I'm sure it will come back," Grace patted his hand reassuringly before pulling both her hands back to herself and tucking them under her legs so she was sitting on them.

"Can I ask you something?" William asked, leaning closer to her.

She paused, the question sounded ominous when said that way. "I suppose so, though I have the right of refusal," she responded, leaning a little forward as well.

"Two coffees," Muriel waited until both William and Grace had pulled away from the table before sliding the coffee cups down. "Are you sure you don't want anything else? Donuts? We have some fresh-made Boston creams?" She was speaking mostly to William.

"No, we're ok, thank you, Muriel." He seemed completely oblivious to her true attentions, and Grace wondered if he was just being polite or if he really was oblivious to all the women who seemed to throw themselves in his line of vision.

"Just let me know," she looked at Grace then back at William before finally turning and walking away.

"She likes you," Grace heard herself before her own mind processed what she said.

William tilted his head down and peered at Grace, "And I like you."

Grace blushed and quickly slid her coffee in front of her. She busied herself with cream and sugar as William's eyes followed her.

"So your big question?" She was so flustered by his statement that she was even willing to bring up the big ominous question herself.

"Ah, yes." He sat back and pulled his own coffee in front of him. He put nothing in it. "I wanted to know. That first time I saw you, you were in the church."

Grace nodded but offered no additional information.

"Well, I've looked for you there ever since then, but I've never seen you."

"I don't go to that church. I don't go to any church, right now." Grace inserted the "right now" quickly. She had gone to church all her life. Every Sunday that she wasn't in church still felt strange.

"Then, why were you there that night?"

Grace put a cool hand up to her warm cheek without taking the other hand out from under her leg.

"Well," she tapped her fingers against her cheek as she thought of an answer that sounded halfway normal. She looked up to William. His eyes were so sincere and understanding, "The thing is... I used to. I prayed for Matthew every day before he died. I trusted his life to God. But, God let me down. He didn't protect my brother. So, I'm having a hard time believing anymore. I don't see how God, the God I knew, could let such a thing happen."

She looked down at the table and closed her eyes. She heard William breathe, but he didn't say anything. After a few seconds, she opened her eyes and looked up at him. He was nodding and thinking.

"I understand," William said. That was all he said. He didn't try to argue the point or to try and find a way to make Matthew's death make sense.

"You were going to a Bible study there?" she asked.

He nodded, "I'm new to the Bible, to belief, and to God. I guess I went into the war without God and came home with him."

"The exact opposite of me," she smiled sadly.

"I have a lot to learn, but it feels right, like I was meant to learn it. I'm sure a lot of men turn to or away from God during the war, but somehow things just lined up the perfect way, in a way that makes me think God is reaching out to *me*, instead of my turning to him." He looked to Grace for confirmation that she understood. She nodded.

"I want to trust again. I want to have faith again." She lifted her coffee cup off the table, it was already getting chilled from the cold cream, and she'd barely had a sip. "I just… can't."

Chapter Twenty-Three

"I can't take you this time," William pleaded with Boy who was barking as William tried to leave. "Ok," William walked back to the kitchen and grabbed a piece of lunchmeat. "You can have this, but you've got to be very good, ok?"

Boy's tail thumped heavily on the floor in anticipation of the meat William held in his hand. William rolled his eyes and smiled at the dog's excitement. He handed the meat to Boy and then made a dash for the door before Boy could realize that William was duping him.

William was saving up enough for a new car, but in the meantime, he had an old sedan that did the trick. He'd washed it up in anticipation of his first real date with Grace. He was still somewhat amazed that she'd actually agreed to go on a real date. They weren't just going for coffee or walking around the town, they were going to dinner. A nice dinner. William had picked an Italian place at the edge of town that Jones had suggested.

William was wearing a suit and tie, and he had picked up a bouquet of white and blue flowers earlier in the day. He hoped he wouldn't put her off by all the attention, but he liked her too much not to think of each piece in the evening.

As he reached her house, William parked the car and picked up the bouquet of flowers. They smelled good. They smelled like Grace. How was it that Grace naturally smelled like a bouquet of freshly picked flowers? It was one of the great mysteries of the world. He smiled at the thought.

William got out of the car and quickly picked off one petal whose edges had turned brown, and then he continued on to the gate.

It felt like some sort of miracle to cross the threshold of the gate. Grace had never let him walk her to the front door before.

When the door opened, Grace was outfitted in a lovely floral dress that pulled into her waist and then flounced out into an easy skirt that moved with the slightest provocation. Her hair was pulled up in a new style. William found that he almost couldn't speak.

"You look stunning," he finally said, to which Grace blushed and smiled. She turned halfway into the house.

"Come in," she moved out of the way for William to walk past her and into the front room.

"These are for you," he held the flowers up to her, and she took them with surprise.

"That is so thoughtful. I'll just run put these in water." She took two steps toward a door along the back wall as another, older woman came out. "Oh, good. William, I want you to meet Ruth," Grace turned to him, but he was staring at the other woman.

It took him a moment to place her. She was in civilian clothes, and in such a different place than the last time he'd seen her, that it was hard for him to put it all together. But his memory was fully intact during that part of his recovery, and he remembered her very well. "Nurse Ruth?"

The woman stopped and stared at William for a long time. William raised his hand and put it over his eye and the part of his face that had been covered by bandages during his stay in her hospital.

"Well, I'll be." Ruth tilted her head. "William Sawyer?"

"You remember my name?" He was shocked. She must have seen hundreds of men during her time abroad, all with wounds, all with names.

"Of course I do. You were with me for a long time and at the end of it all too," Ruth turned. "I think I need to sit down." She moved to an antique chair in the corner. "Well," she said again while looking him over.

"You know each other?" Grace looked to William for an explanation.

"He was in our hospital, just before you got there, or maybe even…" Ruth spoke up. She put her fingers to the bridge of her nose as she tried to remember.

Grace turned to Ruth then back to look at William. She was seeing him with new eyes. His eyes were staring right at her, his mouth partially opened with disbelief.

"Of course," William breathed the words as he stared at Grace. "You were the angel."

Grace was about to ask what he meant by that, but William continued.

"When I first saw you, you were putting medication on that man, the one who was burned down one side of his body? He was so burnt that his skin had practically melted. When I saw you the first time, I thought I was looking at an angel."

"I remember that man," Grace peered at William harder. William watched as she tried to put things together in her mind. Those days were coming back to him. He'd remembered Ruth so well. Ruth had come to talk to him every day. She had been a favorite of all the men. She had sometimes snuck them sweets and let them make bawdy jokes when it made them feel better about being disfigured, maimed, or burned. William had been one of the luckiest ones. His memory might come back, but there was no growing a limb back.

"You memorized those Psalms and recited them to me from heart." William still heard her voice sometimes as he tried to go to sleep. He'd not been able to hold onto her face, but he'd remembered the sweet, calming effect those Psalms had on him. "Thinking of those Psalms put me to sleep for weeks."

Grace's face went white. "I think I need to sit down too."

William smiled, and she laughed as she sat on the sofa where William joined her. "It's unbelievable. It's an impossible coincidence."

"It isn't a coincidence. It can't be." William watched her face move and change with each new thought and feeling that came over her.

"Then what is it?" She looked up at him.

"Providence. Divine providence." It was the only explanation. They had met now because they were meant to meet. God was showing William that this was the woman. His meeting Grace was God's will. A boy from Minnesota and a girl from North Carolina didn't just find each other in Virginia after meeting in a field hospital in the middle of Europe after the war with Germany was over. It had to be God.

Grace shook her head, William could feel her looking for other explanations, but he also knew that she wouldn't find any.

"You always read to me whenever you had time, or you would get someone else to read to me." William turned to Ruth, who was nodding. "You have no idea how much we all appreciated your kindness, how much I appreciated it."

"I remember that old Bible of yours," Ruth smiled. "You could listen all day."

"But you wouldn't read all day," William smiled.

"I remember it," Grace said sitting up. "I remember your Bible too. I remember thinking that it looked just like the Bible I'd gotten as a child. I can't believe I remember that."

"Hmm," Ruth sighed.

"Really?" William turned to Grace with curious eyes. "The funny thing is that it wasn't mine. I have no idea how I got it."

Grace and William stared at each other.

"I don't suppose—Of course it would be impossible." She swallowed as the thought came over her. "Do you think that maybe you knew my brother?"

William shook his head, "I guess it's possible, but there were so many men. Even if it had been his, it isn't likely that I would have known him well."

Grace stood up and walked steadily out of the room. William could see that she was using a good amount of effort to keep herself pulled together. William looked at Ruth, who sat humming and nodding to herself.

When Grace came back into the room, she was carrying a frame. She sat back down next to William with the photo face down on her lap. She lifted the photo and then handed it to William. He carefully took the frame from her, apprehensive about the possibility that he might know Matthew after all.

The photo was of a fair-skinned young man in uniform. The photo was in black and white, so there were things that William couldn't tell about the young man. His face was pleasant, his brow soft. William looked up.

"This is Matthew?" William asked. He hated to disappoint Grace.

Her face changed immediately as she understood what his words meant. He was saying that he didn't know her brother, or if, on the off-chance that he had known him, he couldn't remember it.

William held the photo up again. Those eyes, there was something about the way they were set.

"Were his eyes blue?" William thought back to the map in the night, the scene that had been tucked back into his memory. There in the dark, looking back at him, had been clear blue eyes.

"The bluest you've ever seen," Grace's voice was even. William saw the shade of hope float over her face.

He closed his eyes again. He had been listening for German voices. There was the map next to him and holding the map—the man holding the map…

William looked at Matthew's photo. He remembered eyes clear and as blue as the ocean.

"Was there a tiny scar that ran through his eyebrow?"

There was silence. William looked at Grace. Her face had gone white.

"He was with me. We were in the forest, and he was marking a map for someone." William's words came out slowly. The face formed, and as he stared longer at the photo, the more the man appeared before him.

"Dear me," Ruth put a hand to her chest.

Tears were coursing down Grace's cheeks. She pressed her lips together tightly, and her nostrils flared out as she took in a breath.

"We were friends…Good friends." William felt like his mind was exploding. It was overwhelming, too much. "He, the man I'm seeing, if he's… William stopped at the realization. He looked up at Grace. He had to tell her. "Grace…he stepped in front of a bullet for me. I should have died that night, not him."

Guilt pressed down on his shoulders, swam into his lungs. He could barely look at Grace. She would have her brother here if William had died like he was supposed to. "I think… I need to go lie down for a few minutes," William's voice was raw and shaking. The visions and memories were coming, but they were falling back into his mind too fast, mixing with the guilt that sat fresh in his gut.

"Of course," Ruth stood. Called back into the role of a nurse, she was ready to help. "Come with me," Ruth went to William and took a firm grip on his arm as he stood by her. She led him out of the living room.

He was trying to push the visions from his mind, but they were coming hard and fast and in messy, unorganized order. He didn't even remember getting to the bed, but Ruth sat him down on one.

"Here," Ruth held out a pill and a glass of water. He hadn't noticed her leave or when she'd come back. "This will help you sleep."

William nodded. He needed to sleep. There was too much in his mind. He needed rest. He had to stop the onslaught that was pounding through his mind. He swallowed the pill and lay back onto the bed.

His mind kept churning and swimming with images until finally he was pulled under the hazy sheen of sleep.

~

"He should be out for a few hours at least," Ruth said as she came back into the room where Grace was staring into the opposite wall. Tears were falling down both cheeks in silent coursing streams.

"Are you ok?" Ruth sat down next to Grace and put a thick arm around her shoulders. Grace didn't bother to answer the question put to her.

"It's him, of course it's him…" Grace said in a choked voice.

"What do you mean, sweetie?"

"Matthew wrote to me. He told me that he had a friend and even said his name was William."

"Well, that could be anyone," Ruth rubbed the side of Grace's arm furthest from her.

"But he told me, and I…just missed it. All this time," Grace looked at Ruth. "They said in the letter. The final one. They said he took a bullet for another solider."

Ruth ran a hand up and down Grace's arm and rocked her gently side to side.

"But it was your brother's choice, he chose to give his life," Ruth spoke the words softly into Grace's ear.

"I know," Grace turned to the older woman. "I know."

Chapter Twenty-Four

As the days and nights had gone by, William had remembered more and more. His mind had filled in the details and gaps, and he had begun to see things clearly and in order. He told Grace about the promise he'd made to her brother. He'd sworn that he would visit Matthew's family. Matthew had made him promise.

"Grace, do you think it would be a good idea or a bad one to visit your folks? I don't want to hurt anyone any more than they are already hurt. I'm only asking because it is what he wanted." William looked into Grace's eyes. They were distressed. She'd been shaken since the night she'd discovered Matthew and William's connection.

"I think you should," Grace nodded. "We should do what he wanted," Grace gave a weak smile. "I'll call my parents now."

They took William's car all the way from Charlottesville to Granite Falls. It was a long drive. The two only spoke for the first half of the trip.

When they pulled up to the old, two-story, brown and white house that Grace and Matthew had grown up in, they looked at each other.

"It will be ok," Grace put her hand over William's larger one, and William held her fingers in his. He nodded and released her hand. "Are you ready?" Grace asked with her hand on the door.

William nodded, "Yeah."

The two walked up to the front porch and stared at the front door. Grace took a breath and finally raised her hand to knock.

Her mother opened the door wide. Her eyes went straight to William.

"Mom, this is William Sawyer. William, this is my mother." Ethel stared at William.

"Come in," she said, stepping aside. Grace's father was just inside the living room and stood up as the trio came through.

Once he'd been introduced to William properly, Grace's father gestured to the main chair in the room and said, "Please sit down, William." Grace could see that William was about to decline the chair in deference to her father, but he changed his mind, and she watched her father's head nod approvingly.

William told his story of Matthew beginning to end. He told everything he could remember about Matthew. He left nothing out. He talked about the prayer Matthew gave before the group headed out on their mission and how they'd talked about Christ and his faith before he died. He told them everything up until the moment that Matthew jumped in front of a very deadly, very fast-moving bullet that had been headed straight for William.

As he spoke, he tried his best not to get emotional, but the tears of the family forced him to stop occasionally so he could regain his composure.

After telling them about Matthew's death, he went on to tell them about the Bible he'd found in William's bag, how he'd taken the Bible to bring to Matthew's family, and that it had ended up bringing him to God first.

They all stayed up into the early morning, crying and telling stories about Matthew. His final sacrifice was far from his only sacrifice, as all of the stories showed. Ethel clutched her husband's hand as her jaw shook, and Grace's father pulled her into a tight embrace when she talked about her reaction to Matthew's death.

They all fell into bed as the sun rose. William took the sofa as no one was ready for him to use Matthew's room.

The next day, they slept and ate, told the same stories, stories that had been left out, or stories that had been forgotten, then slept and ate some more.

William and Grace had to head back to Charlottesville after breakfast on the third day. They both had to get back to work even though they would both be too exhausted to be of much use.

Ethel made fluffy pancakes with bacon and eggs as their farewell breakfast feast, and William even saw her smile at her family a few times.

Grace brought William black coffee, and as she handed it to him, she let her hand linger on his.

"Are you going to be ok driving all that way? They say being tired is worse than being drunk," Grace's dad sat with the morning paper unopened next to him.

"Yes sir, I will be just fine." William nodded to the older man.

"If you get tired, you promise me that you will pull over to the side of the road," he said as he pointed a finger at William.

"Of course, *I* could always drive," Grace interjected as her father waited for Ethel to pass the large carafe of orange juice his way.

"You're just as tired, and last I heard, you haven't driven yourself anywhere since you drove our car," her father opened his eyes wide at his daughter in a scolding way. Grace clamped her mouth shut with a faint smile but didn't contradict him.

"Well," Grace said after a moment, "I promise to stay awake with you." She looked at William. "I will make sure you don't fall asleep at the wheel."

"How did the two of you meet in Virginia?" Ethel looked from William to Grace as she piled William's plate with more eggs.

William looked at Grace, and she gave a nod for him to go ahead.

"I was at a Bible study, and suddenly I saw Grace's face just outside the door." As he said it, he could see her perfectly, just as she was then. "I followed her out of the church, but she was already gone."

Ethel gave a little noise of approval.

William thought about that moment and everything that had so easily floated through his head. He hesitated and then took another breath.

"You know what I thought that night, before we'd ever met or been introduced?"

He looked at Grace then at her parents.

"I thought that she was the most beautiful woman I had ever seen…and I wasn't wrong. Then I had this overwhelming feeling. A feeling that I had just seen the woman I was going to marry."

William looked at Grace.

She had a forkful of pancake paused in midair, halfway to her mouth.

Her eyes were fixed on his.

Chapter Twenty-Five

Grace's promise to stay awake with William for the drive back was short-lived. She did her best, which turned out to be one hour, and then she promptly fell into a deep sleep. William liked to see her sleeping next to him. She was so peaceful. His instinct to keep her safe swelled as he watched her steady, soft breath.

He transferred a sleepy Grace back into Ruth's familiar blue house. Boy, who had stayed with Ruth for the three days, nearly knocked William over when he saw him back for the first time.

The next three days were dedicated to sleeping, working, and recovering from the emotionally, physically, and mentally exhausting trip he'd made to North Carolina.

On the fourth day, William went to the hospital and waited outside to walk Grace home. William was frozen in place by the sight of her.

She'd just come off of a twelve-hour shift. She had to be exhausted, but her face was fresh with a pink glow on each cheek. Her eyes lit up at the sight of him, and William could barely grasp the reality of a human being so beautiful.

"You've been waiting for me?" Grace stood planted where she was, and William nodded.

"But no one told me you were here. I wouldn't have taken so long to leave," she turned her head to the side, and William could see that her finely done hair was coming loose from its holdings.

William took a step toward her, "I didn't come in to tell anyone I was here. It's too nice out tonight to go inside anyway." He turned his torso to the sky and the air. Grace walked another step toward him and took in an identical breath in.

When they'd both had their fill of fresh, crisp air, they began walking casually and easily toward Ruth's house. Boy's panting and quick movements were the only thing making noise between them besides the sounds of easy traffic and the night.

"How have you been with everything since you got home?" William's voice was soft, and it matched the feel of the night around them.

Grace thought about the question before answering. "Better. I didn't know how much it would mean for me to know what happened to Matthew, how deeply I needed to know that God hadn't abandoned him out there. He gave his life freely, as impossible as that is to conceive of. His life wasn't ripped from him." She looked at William then back to the town she was walking through.

William mulled over her words.

"I thought that you might not want to see me anymore…once you knew that I'd lived because Matthew died." The thought had been hanging heavily between them. It had begun to cripple William, thoughts slinging themselves at him over and over again since they'd found out about his connection with Matthew.

Grace was quiet for a long time, and then she stopped walking.

"I've been thinking about it a lot. When I first read that he'd been killed, I didn't care that someone else had lived because he died. I just wanted my brother back." She pulled her arms around herself. "But what I've come to realize is that it wasn't my choice. It was Matthew's choice. And he chose the right thing because that is the kind of person he was. I think that without knowing it, he made you our gift from God. He brought us together, and he brought you to help heal my parents and our family."

Grace moved closer to William and looked him straight in the eye, "I don't blame you for being the one he saved. I'm only happy that you *were* the one he saved."

William felt a flush of emotion pull at his heart for the beautiful, kind, and lion-hearted woman who stood before him. Boy gave a pull to move forward.

Grace turned back to the invisible path they'd been walking. They moved in silence as William let Grace's words sink in.

Just before they reached the last turn that would take them to Ruth's house, William pointed down another road that ran parallel to Ruth's.

"Want to go a little bit longer? The leaves are beginning to fall," he looked at the brilliant orange, red, and yellow that lit up the branches of the all the trees lining the block.

Grace smiled and nodded.

They turned down the new street and continued their easy pace as Boy ran side-to-side smelling everything in his path. Today William could understand the impulse. The perfume of fallen leaves mixed with the scent of oncoming fall was intoxicating.

"Grace," William's voice floated down to her like one of the brightly colored leaves. "You should know that what I said at breakfast the other morning, that was true. I knew it from the beginning, and I know it even more now." He looked at Grace, whose face was like a calm, undisturbed water. "I love you. I think I began loving you the day you spoke the Psalms to me, from the moment I saw you as the angel you are."

Grace stopped walking again. Her eyes began to fill despite her calm.

"I want to marry you," William's eyes brushed over her face. He took a ragged breath, "Will you marry me, Grace?"

A fat tear slid down her cheek, and her smile grew.

"If I say yes, then can we go on our fancy date? With a bouquet of flowers, a suit, and car?"

"Is that a yes?" William's heart was aching for an answer. He was aching to love her for the rest of her life.

"Yes," Grace nodded seriously. "That is a yes."

An orange leaf floated down and landed on the side of her hair. William reached out and pushed the small spark of orange away. He leaned forward as he took her face in his hands. He had to bend down to meet her lips, and at the last second, Grace sprang to her toes, wrapped her arms around his neck, and kissed him. Her warm lips pressed against his. William finally let himself wrap his arms all the way around her, and as he lifted her off the ground, her face met his easily.

She felt absolutely perfect in his arms.

~

"And you don't want us to stay with you?" Beau asked as she fluffed her own hair in the one, large mirror in the room.

"I'm just fine," Grace gave each girl a kiss on the cheek and then opened the door for them to all file out.

"Just remember to watch out for the bottom of the skirt. It could trip you. I saw a bride fall down on her wedding day, and it wasn't pretty," Cindy said sternly and then winked at Grace.

"I'll try to remember that. Hey," she asked Katherine, "where is Ginger?"

"Oh, she's with her date," Katherine raised her eyebrows. "The guy with the teeth."

"Really?" Grace didn't realize that she'd miss so much. Katherine nodded vigorously and then left to catch up with the others.

When she closed the door, the room was silent. Grace stood inside the silence just taking it all in for a moment before she headed back to the mirror.

Grace looked at herself over. Her mother's pearls hung from her neck. Her gown was satin, the color of moonlight, with long sleeves with tons of buttons going up them and up the back. And there was a soft, lovely flare at the bottom. Her father would be coming to get her soon. She'd wanted just a few moments alone before making her way down the aisle and into the rest of her life as Mrs. William Sawyer.

Moving her eyes from the mirror, she walked herself to the window and sat on one of the small children's chairs that were the only places to sit in this Sunday school classroom.

Grace carefully folded her hands and bowed her head.

"Lord," her voice issued into the quiet of the room. "I just wanted to say *thank you* before I make this journey. Thank you for sticking with me even when I was walking away from you. Thank you for William and all that he's brought to my life. I didn't think this would be a part of my life after we lost Matthew, but now I have the love of this wonderful man for the rest of my life." She paused.

"Also, if Matthew is there with you, Lord, let him know that I am all right. Show him what you did with his gift and maybe…if you want to… let him be on the other side of me as I walk down the aisle today."

Grace looked up at the sound of a knock on the door.

"Thank you," she whispered before she stood to get the door for her father.

~

The organ music began, and the main doors to the sanctuary opened. Grace watched as all the guests stood and turned to look at her.

Grace felt her father's arm securely beneath her own. She took her first steps down the aisle and felt an abundant burst of love for every person in the room.

William's eyes were taking her in. She felt again how incredibly blessed she was to love a man who could look right into her soul just by the love he gave her.

Ruth was sitting next to her mother, and Grace smiled at them both. Ginger and her new beau were standing side-by-side, he a good foot taller than her. Cindy, Beau, and Katherine all stood together as Cindy motioned for Grace to watch that she didn't trip over her skirt. Even Millie from her old field hospital days had made the trip especially for her.

William's mother and grandmother were both crying tears of joy in the front row. Grace was thankful for them both and impatient to get to know them better. Jones and his family were in their Sunday best, with even the littlest baby wearing a special flouncy gown.

As Grace took another step toward William, she felt her foot catch on her hem. She would have thought of Cindy if gravity hadn't been taking all of her attention and suddenly tugging her downward.

Her father's grip tightened on her right arm, but she felt something else.

With another step, she regained her footing and looked up to see William smiling broadly for the disaster that had been averted. As she righted herself completely, she also felt her heart squeeze. As she'd been about to fall forward, she'd felt herself being lifted from her left side as well.

Grace paused to suck in a quick breath and keep herself from crying. Before she moved forward again, Grace let her eyes move quickly to her left. With a swell of love, Grace thanked God. For though there was nothing to see, her heart knew better.

A note to my readers

I really appreciate you taking the time to read my book and I would like to thank you from the bottom of my heart. If you enjoyed the story, please leave a review where you purchased the book. You'll be helping others make a decision on their purchase and I appreciate your effort, so will other forthcoming readers. If you would like to be the first to know about my new releases, promotions and giveaways, please sign up for my mailing list here. If you have any comments or questions about my books, please do not hesitate to contact me at katherinesaintclair@gmail.com.

Katherine St. Clair

More books from Katherine St. Clair

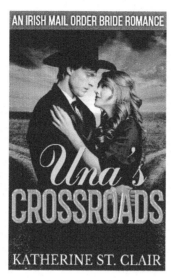

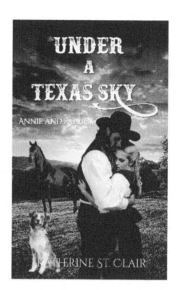

Made in the USA
Las Vegas, NV
05 December 2022